HOW TO WIN AT LIFE

...BY CHEATING AT EVERYTHING!

AN ILLUSTRATED GUIDE TO ALL THINGS
FROM CONNING YOUR WAY THROUGH HIGH SCHOOL TO BILKING A SMALL TOWN

WRITTEN BY **MARK PEREZ** ILLUSTRATIONS BY **SCOTT SHAW!**
PHOTOS BY **ANNASTASIA GOLDBERG**

Publisher
Mike Richardson

Editor
Jemiah Jefferson

Designer
Anita Magaña

Special thanks to Keith Goldberg at Dark Horse Entertainment.

Published by
Dark Horse Books
A division of Dark Horse Comics, Inc.

Dark Horse Comics
10956 SE Main St.
Milwaukie, OR 97222
DarkHorse.com

Names: Perez, Mark, auhor. | Shaw, Scott, illustrator. | Goldberg,
  Annastasia, photographer.
Title: How to win at life ... by cheating at everything : an illustrated
  guide to all things: from conning your way through high school, to bilking
  a small town / written by Mark Perez ; illustrations by Scott Shaw ;
  photographs by Annastasia Goldberg.
Description: Milwaukie, OR : Dark Horse Books, [2017]
Identifiers: LCCN 2016049407 (print) | LCCN 2016053233 (ebook) | ISBN
  9781506701943 (paperback) | ISBN 9781630089832
Subjects: LCSH: Swindlers and swindling--Fiction. | Conduct of life--Fiction.
  | Satire. | BISAC: FICTION / Humorous. | FICTION / Satire.
Classification: LCC PS3616.E74337 H69 2017 (print) | LCC PS3616.E74337
  (ebook) | DDC 813/.6--dc23
LC record available at https://lccn.loc.gov/2016049407

First Dark Horse Books Edition: June 2017
10 9 8 7 6 5 4 3 2 1
Printed in The United States of America

TABLE OF CONTENTS

This book is dedicated to my father. A man who taught me that the best things in life are free. Especially when you can swindle them off of somebody else.

FOREWORD

S teal this book. Yep. You read that right. Don't pay for it with your Discover card. Don't download a cheaper version on your Kindle. This one—this actual book that's in your hands right now—put it in your pocket and steal it. Because—here's the thing—if you pay for this book and *then* read it, it would totally defeat the purpose of why I wrote it in the first place. So have some balls for once in your miserable excuse for a life. Grab the goddamned book. Jam it into your purse or down the front of your pleated Dockers or under your uglier-than-average kid's stroller, and walk right out that front door. Don't be a pussy. DO IT! NOW! GO! *GO!*

Okay, everybody calm down. I'm just joking. But now that I have your attention, I can explain my reason for writing this book in the first place. Because I'm sure you're wondering, "Why the hell would a master of his craft, at the height of his powers, decide to publicly divulge all of his trade secrets?" They say Houdini went to his grave with every one of his tricks. And like a magician, or a psychiatrist, or Bruce Jenner's cadre of plastic surgeons, the con man is sworn to a code of confidentiality—to never disclose the secrets that have been passed down from generation to generation, mentor to apprentice, or, as it was in my case, father to son.

But fortunately for you, and unfortunately for me, I am dying.

Therefore, I have decided that before I do expire, as a sort of penance for all the shitty stuff that I have perpetrated in this life (and I have perpetrated quite a bit of shitty stuff, as you'll soon read), I am going to pool the resources in my mind and put all of that knowledge down on paper. I want this book to act as not only a testament of my life, but also as a sort of guidebook to yours, illuminating the darker part of our society, where it's getting harder lately to delineate what's *right* from what's *wrong*.

Now, how this book is used—well, that's up to you. As soon as you crack this book open to chapter 1, I wash my hands of what happens next. It's kinda like posting a bomb-making recipe on the Internet. If you're a civilian trying to understand the mind of a lunatic, you'll use it to know how to protect yourself from those who want to kill you by making a bomb. But if *you're* the lunatic, then I suspect I just helped you make one.

Also worth noting: all proceeds from this book will go to a foundation I recently created, the Coalition Helping Underprivileged and Moneyless Peoples. A nonprofit organization that remunerates the most vulnerable casualties of fraudulence in this country. The old, the very young, and the underrepresented. You see, folks, if I can somehow pay back society, even just a little, for all the ills I have caused it, then my life will not have been lived in vain.

My dear, departed father once told me, "To know even one life has breathed easier because you have lived—this is to have succeeded." Well, this one's for you, Dad.

In closing, I'd just like to say that all of the previous is total bullshit. I'm not dying. I have no interest in helping anyone, let alone giving some saps back their fucking money. And the Coalition Helping Underprivileged and Moneyless Peoples is something I just made up literally two minutes ago. My father gave me a lot of advice growing up, most of it terrible. But it was Ralph Waldo Emerson who said that ridiculous quote about helping others. Barf. Oh, and the acronym for my fake charity is actually CHUMP—because I'm clever.

I guess that's my point. The real lesson to be learned here has already been taught. In the last few seconds, just by reading the mere foreword to this book, you have already been scammed. And that's the thing. It's just that easy. And in the succeeding pages, I'm gonna show you just *how* easy. Now, what the hell are you doing here? Reading this foreword in the middle of the store like a jerkoff?

HOW TO STEAL THIS BOOK

Hide it in a place no sane person
would ever want to frisk.

Grab a much cheaper book.
Perhaps about dieting?

Pretend you forgot to pay for said diet book
you're never *ever* gonna read.

Pay for the cheaper book. When the alarm
sounds again, they will inevitably let your
fat ass walk right out the door with your
ironic weight-loss book in tow.

Steal the fucking book.

Note: If you've got real *cojones*, you'd *also* return the stolen book after you're done
reading it and get "your" money back. That's the move. But first things first . . .

PART 1:

BECOMING THE WORST PERSON YOU CAN BE!

START CHEATING NOW—READ THE LAST CHAPTER FIRST

My plan working to perfection.

This is your first lesson about any great racket or scheme. **You *always* start at the end.** When you do that, when you *start* where you want to *finish*, then you'll always know how it's going to turn out—well before it actually does. And that is key in this Game of Con. Always know the results ahead of time. In a boxing match. In a presidential election. In life. I mean, think about it: what if you could gauge how *everything* ended before it *actually* did? And imagine if you could do that with all the important moments in your life. Look into the future to see how things turned out, years ahead of time. For example:

What if you could see just how enormous your beautiful wife was going to balloon up to some twenty years after you married her?

Wouldn't it be great to see the dead-end your "promising job" was going to lead to before you devoted some thirty-five fucking years of your life to that pointless tripe?

And just imagine if you could see the galactic loser your sweet bundle of joy would turn out to be—before you spent a couple hundred thousand dollars and the best years of your life raising his ridiculously disappointing ass?

Well, the same is true when you're trying to pull off one of the biggest, most ambitious cons in the history of the art form. At the end of the day, a great con is not just about stealing millions of dollars via some underground computer hack (any egghead with no imagination can do that). No, this con was less about the size of the haul—and more about the *scope* of the crime. I had made enough loot. This was going to be the kind of swindle that would be talked about for years in the annals of con-dom (not the Trojan kind). Now, *that's* what I was after. A certain level of immortality. And as you'll see by reading this book, not only will I teach you the basics, but if you pay close attention, maybe take some notes in the margins, I might just show you how to steal an entire town.

And if you're really, *really* good, after you've scammed them all, you may even end up beloved there.

I'm sure when you were little, there was some asshole adult figure in your life—a guidance counselor, a Big Brother, maybe even a super flirty priest—who told you some bullshit about "keeping your feet on the ground and reaching for the stars." Or maybe that was Casey Kasem. Either way, it's all garbage. "Trying your best" and "never giving up on your dreams" will usually lead to living a life well below the poverty line and playing rhythm guitar for a Maroon 5 cover band at Universal CityWalk. The only, and let me repeat that, *only* way to succeed in this life is to cheat. You don't believe me? Henry Ford became an industrial success *in good part* because he sold to both sides during World War II (and yes, one of those sides was the fucking Nazis). Joseph Kennedy basically *bought* the US presidency for his son by using the immense profits from a very illegal bootlegging operation. And New York billionaire Leona Helmsley was once quoted as saying, "We don't pay taxes. Only the little people pay taxes." (A New York federal court disagreed—and gave her eighteen months in prison, by the way.) And while Leona was an asshole for actually saying it out loud—the witch was right.

You see, I wrote this book not only to prove that anybody can become a con man, but also, and more importantly, that *most* extremely successful people are con men in their own right. I also wanted to show that the greatest con man in the world (hello, me) could accomplish anything if he put his mind to it. And not by reaching for the stars. Or being all I could be. But by using the library of skills I'm about to lay out for you, in detail, in the following pages. Which means you too can accomplish anything. You can con a whole town. And get rich while doing it. And, if you do it properly . . . you *may* even achieve something greater.

Because at the end of the day, this book is about *winning at life*. About getting every-thing you ever dreamed of. And oddly enough, it's a sort of love story, too. About two people you'd never imagine would end up together in the end . . . ending up together in the end. So now that you *know* how the story ends, how's about we get back to where it begins . . .

COMMITTING CRIMES AS A TODDLER

I stole my first car when I was three. That's not a typo, folks. *Three.* Now, while I didn't pull off the scam entirely by myself, I was certainly a semi-willing accomplice, or at least as willing as you can be, committing grand theft auto while still in pre-K. One of the first lessons to learn is that everything and everyone around you can always be used as potential tools to aid you in a **grift**. Maybe it's a **Michigan roll** (a few dollar bills wrapped around a roll of Xerox paper). Maybe it's a **cackle-bladder** (a squib of red dye you bite down on when you fake a slip-and-fall at Home Depot). Or maybe it's one of the most commonly used tools in **the Game**: a **shill**, also known as a **capper** (a seemingly innocent accomplice that makes people feel more comfortable when dealing with a total stranger—you).

It could be a dog with one leg. It could be an older person with a broken-down walker. Or it could be, as was the case in my first foray into the Game, a toddler.

People are generally trusting. I have no idea why that is. With all the history of cheating and deceiving that has been perpetrated over time, by individuals, religions, and just about every government that has ever existed on Earth, you'd think a healthy skepticism would have been ingrained in us, merely by natural selection. But luckily for guys like me, humankind remains genetically naive—dumb fuckers who may walk on two feet but still think like their ape ancestors. And sometimes all they need is a little push back to their more natural position: bent over on all fours.

Here's a quick list of quality shills and cappers:

THE ELDERLY

Our country has decided to collectively deem old people useless and a burden on our society. I am here to tell you that notion is some totally ageist bullshit. I'll agree that they're super depressing to look at, and tend to repeat the same fond memories of the Korean conflict and institutionalized racism, but they do have a purpose in this world. A worthwhile function. A reason for taking that *very* dubious first breath every morning. And that purpose is to help you get over on somebody. Even if they're unaware of it at the time. *Especially* if they're unaware. Which is what makes being a **confidence man** a true art form. Any asshole can storm into a bank and rob the joint with an ironic mask and a half-decent sub-machine gun. But it takes a true artisan to enter that same bank armed only with an octogenarian in a wheelchair and take the place for triple what the *Point Break* guys made off with. So make friends with an oldie. You'll find it makes suffering through those long, boring stories about how the Hollywood Jews faked the moon landing well worth it.

ANIMALS

There's a reason that you may see thousands of people die in a disaster movie, but you *almost never* see a single dog killed. And that's because the powers that be know that people love dogs far more than they love each other. And although that may seem irrational and unsettling, think of it this way: Humans cheat, they murder, they pretend to have a debilitating back injury in order to receive a government check. Meanwhile, all a dog wants from you is love. Kinda makes sense when you think of it that way, doesn't it? Now, choosing *any* animal won't do. You need to pick just the right one. If you're gonna bilk an old lady, usually a tabby cat works best. If you're gonna roll a meathead with a tribal tattoo, buy an obnoxiously large snake. And if you plan on duping your average Middle American rube, *always* go with a dog, preferably a puppy. (Note: Never use a parrot. You'll come off as the weird guy at the party that people expect to start juggling bowling pins. Unless you're trying to roll a pirate. Then it's apropos.)

FOREIGNERS

I know what you're thinking. *Foreigners???* We're Americans, damn it. Americans have hated foreign-ers since the Pilgrims docked their cruise ship on Plymouth Rock and gave the natives syphilis and a hastily written eviction notice. This is all true, of course, but there are always exceptions to any rule. Generally speaking, foreigners can be divided into two categories, easily understood for your mildly racist American consumption. For example . . .

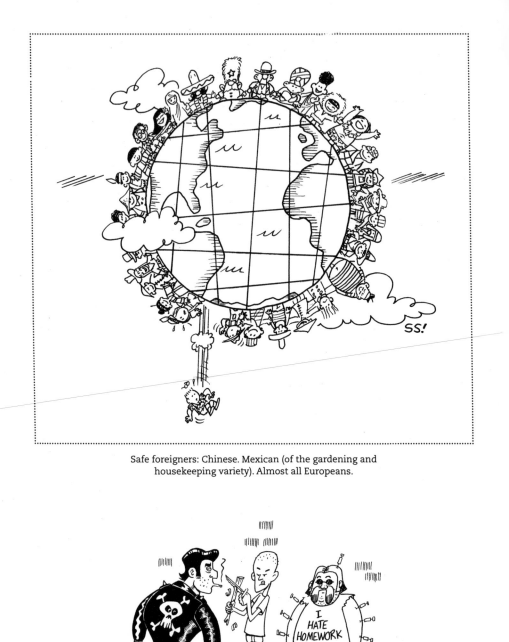

Safe foreigners: Chinese. Mexican (of the gardening and housekeeping variety). Almost all Europeans.

Dangerous foreigners: Middle Eastern. Mexican (of the gangbanging variety). And Russian.

You know those commercials? Where they show you some starving African kid from Malawi eating a handful of dust for breakfast? And then that fat, bald guy starts in with the whole "for just forty cents a day" rap, making you feel all terrible while you're eating a bacon double cheeseburger and chili fries in front of your plasma TV? Well, it's *that* same effect that you want to produce when you are perpetrating a ruse of this kind. I'm telling you, just as an experiment, go walk into any church accompanied by a skinny kid with terrible teeth from war-torn Burundi (or some other similarly shitty locale), and you'll see just how quickly you'll be getting donations to pay for the make-believe college he's never going to attend.

And finally, that brings us to . . .

CHILDREN

There is nothing, and I repeat, *not one thing* that works better at getting close to people than the sights and sounds of an innocent child. Me, personally, I hate kids. Always have. (Really they're just shorter, more selfish versions of adults. And as you will clearly see, I already despise adults.) But I *will* stomach using a kid for an afternoon because the results are usually well worth it. When you're entering the **sting phase** (the final stages of a con), no matter what the cheat is, carrying a baby on your arm works as a sort of shield. A vomiting, poopy-diaper-producing precautionary measure that can help you achieve your goals. And if you want to tweak those results? Make it a Filipino or a black baby. And if you really wanna go for broke, put some of those *Forrest Gump*–style polio crutches on that little fucker. People will be falling over themselves to help you steal money from them. And that's exactly how my old man used me, God rest his soul.

I don't really remember every aspect of the scam that day, back when I helped my degenerate father steal a car. But I do remember the car: a 1984 Pontiac Fiero. Believe it or not, that was a very desirable car that year. (Note: Never name a car "Fiero" when it has a predilection for catching fire for absolutely no reason.) Anyway, I do recall my dad's reaction after I helped him— pure elation. And I remember what he told me

that day. He said, "Son, you just witnessed a very valuable lesson here today. People are really fucking stupid. Which means you only need to be just slightly less stupid than the rest of society in order to take advantage of it. Now, get your goddamned gimp braces off the dashboard, dipshit. This is a brand new car."

Some kids think of their first hit in T-ball as the primary step into boyhood, while others think of their First Communion as a major spiritual milestone. As for me, I think of my first grift as a sort of scammer's bar mitzvah (again, this was grand theft auto, age three, in case you forgot). While I'm sure many of you reading this are suddenly feeling sorry for me, that feeling . . . that pinch in your gut that tells you it's all wrong . . . *that* is why all of the information I gave you above works. People like to feel sorry for others. Not because they give half a shit about you or me, not even a little. Rather, they enjoy feeling superior. And that's because human beings are innate narcissists. Take this as a truism about the world, and then use it to your advantage.

HOW TO USE A BABY TO STEAL A CAR

Find or make-your-own handicapped baby.

Always choose a two-seater car.

Insist on having your gimp son ride shotgun during the test drive, because of his tendency towards violent grand mal seizures.

Test drive the car all the way home and don't forget to change the plates.

Always keep this in mind when performing a **shell game** (any deceit, swindle, or fraud). When you can keep it simple, keep it simple. Don't get all complicated for complicated's sake. Because things will usually go sideways on their own, and you'll be better off not having a laundry list of shit to keep straight in your head.

As I grew older, I became a more willing participant in my dad's "career," like being a batboy for the Yankees when your dad plays right field, or a stage-hand when your father sits first violin in the New York Philharmonic. Being around the best may not make you the best, but it will certainly give you a head start. (Ten thousand hours of practice to make a true genius, as they say.) And that's exactly what I got: a head start. I took the things my dad gave me (you know, in lieu of love and security and any emotional connection whatsoever) and used them to get me through that awful, terrible, miserable human experience we romantically refer to as "growing up." You see, everything I learned was taught to me by my father, C. F. Frost. (Sound familiar? That's the dummy name they put on sample Amex cards, and not *actually* my dad's name.) C. F. gave me an in-depth tutorial in how to get over on civilians, from grade school teachers to college deans, from Health and Human Services employees to schoolyard bullies. It wasn't necessarily a Hallmark-type childhood.

But who are we kidding—what childhood really is? The majority of kids are either being molested by their "cool uncle" or beaten up for having a Jewy-sounding last name. And that's because being young isn't all *Star Wars*–themed birthday parties and memorable summer camp shenanigans. It fucking sucks for the most part. So better to grasp that early in life, rather than trying in vain to live some impossible Disneyesque fantasy.

Now, as for me, when your mom dies before you turn two, and the only secure adult figure in your life is carrying around more felonies than disposable diapers, you tend to end up just a wee bit screwed up. But I'm not here to cry for myself. My dad could have very easily dropped me off at an orphanage (like I would have done, by the way). Instead, he decided to teach me (and use me in) all of his con games. And I guess, looking back, that was the only thing he knew how to do. What else could he pass on to me? His love of stamp collecting? His passion for Civil War reenacting? Zzzzzzz. All of that shit sounds pretty fucking terrible anyway, if you ask me. So Pops may not have been big on hugs. Or outward affection. Or being my actual father. But the old bastard was passionate about *The Game*. And that's something he passed down to me with fervor. Which is a lot more than you can say about most dads. So I guess, at the very least, I'm grateful to him for that.

Anyway, Dad and I moved around a lot—the result of stealing money from almost every human being we came into contact with. Believe it or not, I attended over one hundred different schools. Let me restate that numerically so it's very clear: *100 different schools*. And along the way I acquired a few lessons that may or may not be helpful to you. School for me was more than a place to study geometry, chemistry, and all the other shit you will *never* use again in your fucking life. No, to me it was a testing ground for my bullshit, a control group on which to hone my craft, an ideal place to perfect some tangible real-world skills, like charm, cunning, and the ability to read body language. Mastering how to manipulate the unwitting and make them do my personal bidding. Discovering the best ways to cheat the less clever out of positions and possessions that I, in turn, wanted for myself. So in that regard, those one hundred various "workshops" I enrolled in really *were* "schools" after all. From which I received a unique type of education. The kind that would actually benefit me in the future. All pieces in the puzzle that would (unknown to me at the time) eventually lead me to a CON FOR THE AGES. And all this shit can be plenty helpful to you, too, in what I can only assume is your own boring, average life. So, as Pops would say, "Pay attention here, dipshit. This part's important."

FELONIES FOR GRADE SCHOOLERS, AGES 6 AND UP

My dad always used to say something else to me that was rather poetic: "Son, you're never too young to start taking advantage of those less fortunate than you." And I used it as a mantra throughout the years between kindergarten and the sixth grade. I always knew that I wasn't going to be at any one school for more than a couple of weeks, so I could pull off things that the poor schmucks who had to stay for the duration of their scholastic careers could never get away with themselves. That being said, here are a few musts for you youngsters out there who want to follow in my footsteps:

BE HELD BACK

When enrolling at a new school, always hold yourself back at least three years. I know that seems counterintuitive to the main tenets of the pathetic helicopter parenting of today, with kids being pushed forward a grade or two by overzealous mothers and fathers insecure about their own limited abilities and shortcomings. But in the world of grift, being smarter, bigger, and wiser than your peers is a table you will always try to set, no matter how old you are. I enrolled in the sixth grade thirty-seven times. Given this, it's reasonable to conclude that each time I got bigger, smarter, and better at the sixth grade, right? Of course I did! And that's because all the other kids feared me. All the teachers were impressed by me. And I was always the first pick at recess. Every. Fucking. Time. And *that's* why this move is a no-brainer.

BE BLIND

Don't listen to those sensitive Marys who will tell you otherwise; there are a lot of benefits to being severely disabled in grade school. The faculty feels sorry for you, so your workload is next to nil. They usually assign some poor sap to carry your books and buy your lunch. This is tantamount to having a young slave, which is always nice. But most importantly, when your dad has

you sneaking into the teachers' lounge and rooting around in their lockers for cash and other valuables, you always have an airtight alibi: "Hey asshole, can't you see that I'm fucking blind? I am a totally blind child! With two dead eyes!!" You will win that argument every time, *sight unseen* (thank you, please tip your waitress).

BE A MINORITY

Now this one is a little tricky. You go to the *wrong* school with this particular hustle, and you may find a large pride of toothless parents picketing outside for you to be bused back to where you *done come'd from*. But if you choose the *right* school, like Dear Old Dad always did, there are a lot of rewards to being an oppressed minority. You see, here

are the statistical facts: About half the country is racist. And the other half feels guilty about the previous half. So if you go to a school in a neighborhood that feels guilty . . . for some reason, magically, your lunch gets paid for. Don't ask me why, but it just does. Also, you can kind of do no wrong there. Everyone automatically assumes that you're from a broken home, or that your dad regularly hits you with a switch, or any other cliché they've seen on basic cable. So you're afforded some extra leniency to do whatever your little ethnic heart desires, which is most likely something illegal.

DIE

Almost every time I left a school, I died. I was either run over by a drunk driver or drowned in a cousin's aboveground pool. I was even hit by lightning (twice, ironically). And don't believe what they say about a short life; there are a lot of benefits to dying young. For one thing, people will send you food. Well, not *you*—your father. And I'm talking a *lot* of food. We would eat for a month afterward on the offerings of others. Good food, too. Also, in lieu of flowers, the sad mourners are admonished to donate in your name to a specific charity—one that just happens to run its funds through your father's many personal bank accounts. An ironic thing about the world: People generally treat you like total shit while you're alive, but the minute you're dead, their generosity toward you knows no bounds. It's one of the great mysteries of the universe. So again, capitalize on that shit.

A key element to running a successful operation is to be light and mobile. To always be on to the next thing before the present thing is on to you. And if you're a relatively smart **ripper**, the only way you'll get pinched is if you stick around the scene of the crime like some creepy serial killer peeking over the police tape at his latest triple homicide. My father and I traversed the entire continental US. We worked our racket in literally every one of the contiguous United States, as well as Alaska. And I learned that as big a country as America is, there's a different *class* of people everywhere you look. Think about it: the United States is equal in size to all of Western Europe. So you can imagine that in it there would be as distinct and disparate a set of cultures as you would find in, say, France, Germany, or England. And *within* said cultures, there are a few basic principles that will help you to blend into the local customs and consuetudes.

For example . . .

If we're ever lucky enough to see an actual end-of-days reckoning like they keep promising us, Montana is where a new dystopian civilization will rise from the ashes like a retarded phoenix. There are more neoconservative, ultra-right-wing, concealed-carrying, nuclear-bunker-owning residents in Big Sky Country than there are snow-topped mountain peaks. So if you want to get in good with the local community, have a visceral distrust of the Federal Government and wear that paranoia on your sleeve (of the ridiculous militia uniform your very weird neighbor just made you). That kind of thing will get you far in the Treasure State.

Florida is a bit complex when it comes to culture (or lack thereof). The state is equally split into three terrible parts: the Panhandle, or as those in the know like to call it, the Redneck Riviera (not the best moniker), located in the northern part of the state yet considered part of the Deep South. Caution: beware here if your skin is of a tinted hue. Then there's Central Florida. Obviously located in the center of Florida, it is filled with so many overweight fanny-packers, you might as well be in Ohio. Aside from Cape Canaveral, we should just give this entire section back to Spain. And speaking of Spain, if you want to work an angle in South Florida, you'd better start working on your Spanish first, because you're going to need it down there, señor.

We'll call these "the Friendly States." Most of the people that live here are simple. And by *simple*, I mean *dumb*. You don't live in Iowa or Minnesota because you're "chasing a dream" or because you plan to "light the world on fire" with your revolutionary thinking. No, you live there because you're too much of an idiot to know that some states have a beach. Have you ever been to Minnesota? It's cold three hundred days a year up in that flat icebox. If I lived there, the first time it snowed in September, I'd move. I don't care if my entire family had lived there for three hundred fifty years. I'd move *that day*. The September snow day. As far as I'm concerned, this is the Motherland of Cons. All those rubes packed into the welcoming plains of Middle America like wounded deer in a canned hunting pen. Just waiting to be whacked. This area of the map is a great place to run a **country send** (when you roll a rube for everything he's got, and then just a little bit more—because you can). This is the only reason you would ever catch me there.

I like to call this area "Hickistan" or "the United States of Racism." The millions of crackers who populate this area are still pissed off that they lost the war. And by *war*, I don't mean Vietnam. I mean Civil. (Confederate Memorial Day is an actual holiday that they celebrate here. Where state employees get the day off. You know, in memoriam of that little "Let's Save Slavery" conflict that they lost.) So don't feel bad when you take from these proud Hickistani assholes. Just remember two things: Be smarter than they are, which isn't too difficult. And also be super white.

It's necessary to keep all these things in mind when you're starting your *new* life, *alone* at a very young age, much like I was about to do. You see, as weird as my upbringing with my father was, you have to remember that up to this point, he was my only *real* connection to anybody. Every other human being that I had ever come into contact with was objectified in my mind as a mark, a dupe, or a sucker. My old man, as socially perverse and fucked up as he was, was my only grounded connection to reality. He was the alpha and the omega in my life. Oh, and he was also a tremendous fucking dumbass. Always way too greedy. Often way too careless. Always doing something more-than-questionable that would affect me in the short term, as you will soon see. But on this occasion, he did something that would also teach me a grand lesson in the long run.

And that lesson is: never get too attached to anybody in your life. Your wife. Your dog. Your dad. Because in this life, the only guarantee you get is that someday, they will *all* leave you. Your wife will run off with her masseuse. Your dog will get hit by a car. And your dad . . . My dad . . . Well, let's just say someway, somehow, one day you will look up, and that "important person" in your life will be gone. And there is nothing you can do about it. And that's a fact of life that can never be altered, abridged, or avoided. And those are God's rules, not mine. So take it up with him.

GETTING YOUR VARSITY LETTER IN FLEECING

Higsh school was a strange time for me. But who am I kidding? It's a strange time for everyone, right? I just mean it was even stranger than most. You see, around that time, my dad got pinched by the Feds. And subsequently, he got slapped with a good chunk of time for running a **badge play**. (That's when you impersonate a cop, generally by writing phony tickets, eating for free, etc. But Pops, in his ultimate wisdom, had decided to make a major drug bust. Which was then picked up by the local papers. Which then put him up for a commendation. The only problem was that . . . he wasn't an actual fucking cop! So Pops got *popped*.) I never forgave him for disappearing from my life that day. But, as it turns out, I made the best of it. You see, the greatest lessons in life often seem the most cruel. From that point on, I was forced to stay at the same school for longer than usual. Which was completely foreign to me. For the first time, I was compelled to use my skills on the *same* people. With no exit strategy. No getaway plan. No degenerate dad to help cover my ass. I couldn't just pick up and run if it got too hot. My old man told me to hang tight until he figured a way out of his mess, which, as it turned out, would take much more time than either of us expected. So there I was. Alone. Stuck. Totally unmoored. And of all the things my dad had done to me . . . all the shams he used me in . . . all the precarious spots he'd put me in . . . this was the one I would never forgive him for.

Anyway, my sophomore year I attended Central Valley High in Sunnytown, California (not the real name of either, FYI). There I gathered quite a bit of knowledge on how to game the system while being *inside* the system: how to get perfect grades without ever cracking open a book, how to make varsity teams in spite of having no athletic ability whatsoever, and how to rob freshman girls of their virginities while never *once* having to use force (I'm staunchly against rape, also an FYI). And lucky for you, I'm about to share how. So let's start with . . .

REPUTATION

There are four places to make a name for yourself:

Scoring on the field.

Scoring in the classroom.

Scoring in the ring.

Scoring in the back of
a 2004 Hyundai Sonata.

HOW TO BE THE BMOC

Having a reputation can mean many things. If you're going to a WASPy, entitled-rich-kid school, rep starts and ends with your transcripts. Nowadays this may be a bit more complicated to pull off, with computers and digital records and the like, but in my day, all you needed was some whiteout, a typewriter, and the number to a phony high school. ("Hello, Sweet Valley High, Office of the Registrar. Can I help you?")

Conversely, if you have the misfortune of going to a more *difficult* school, and by *difficult* I mean one of color and/or a diverse ethnicity, you're better off carrying a different kind of rep from your fake previous school. Like being a person of interest in a homicide case and/or some questionable family ties to *la Cosa Nostra*. This is a crucial lesson, so commit it to memory: know the game you're going to be playing before you show up with your ball. For example, my high school was a little Bible Belty, so I became the son of a preacher, complete with good grades and a two-year mission of bringing the Word of the Lord to some miserable third-world country that I randomly picked off a map. (By the way, why do these pious pricks always bring the Word of the Lord to starving kids? How about a hoagie? Or a nonstop plane ticket to a Carl's Jr.? Anyway, I digress.)

The initial place to stake out is the hub of all high-school socialization . . .

THE CAFETERIA

The cafeteria can be quite a terrifying place, especially for the new kid. But there are a few ways to make this experience a bit more tolerable. The first thing to do is to think of high school as prison and the cafeteria (as it is in an *actual* prison) as where all the important shit goes down. Where a new inmate makes a name for himself. Perhaps by shanking a shot-caller or keistering a bag of heroin inside his lower digestive tract or figuring out a way to take down a corrections officer. Believe it or not, high school has a "junior varsity" version of these *exact* penal situations. Allegorically speaking. If you want to make a name for yourself from grades nine through twelve, I would recommend doing it in the lunchroom, and, more specifically, engaging in one of the following activities to get your high-school career off on the right foot:

SELL WEED

If you want to make friends fast, and I mean *really* fast, don't be known as the kid with the great personality. Be known as the kid with the great herb. Remember, you're not doing this to make a profit. That's the short game. The long game is to make relationships with all the power brokers of the school: The jocks. The preps. The geeks. The stoners.

And remember, this isn't 1975 anymore, *you dig?* Nowadays *all* of these groups regularly partake in a myriad of cannabis goods, and they enjoy them even more at a discount. And since you could give two shits if you get caught and it gets put on your record (a record that is already fake to begin with, mind you), you can quickly become the Tony Montana of grade ten. The word *con* is short for *confidence*, and in every scam, you are trying to gain the confidence of strangers. And nothing helps you gain the confidence of sixteen- and seventeen-year-olds like selling them fat blunts for a steal.

BEAT UP THE BULLY

This is also a classic axiom of prison life, one that holds true to high-school hierarchy as well. There is no quicker way to the top of the social ladder than if you find the biggest, baddest motherfucker on campus and lay him out on his ass for all to see. However, this can also be a little tricky to pull off. For instance, paying the captain of the football team to take a dive could totally backfire on you. A couple of things could go wrong in this scenario. Puffed up by the chanting of the cafeteria mob, Tommy Linebacker might change his mind at the last minute and decide to

beat your ass anyway. Or, even if he *does* take the dive, as you stand over him victorious, like Ralph Macchio at the 1984 All Valley Karate Championships, his buddies could look for some immediate Cobra Kai retribution. Next thing you know, you're in the hospital, drinking meatloaf through a straw and blinking answers to your doctors' questions.

So to lessen the chances of these negative outcomes, I recommend that you cast the part of the bully. That's right: you hire a guy to start school around the same time as you. Have him show up at lunch one day; if you're inventive like me, you forge his transcripts, too, just like you did your own. He should be huge, about twenty or so, and should terrorize the school for a good week or two before you put your plan into action. Then you set your stage. Let your stooge know exactly what's going to go down like it was a WWE pay-per-view. It usually works like this: The stooge enters the cafeteria and begins to pick on numerous students (particularly the Asian exchangers and the fat kids), shoving them, stealing their lunch money, or some other odious equivalent most of us are all too familiar with. Then, after making the rounds, the stooge ends up meeting you at his preordained mark—in the middle of the lunch tables. Center stage. Lights, camera, action. Right in front of the entire school. Be sure to pick a high-traffic time. Make sure he's got a cackle-bladder in his mouth (that fake blood packet I mentioned earlier). And let him call you every name in the book, maybe even knock you down a few times if you really feel like pushing the production value. And then get up, like you've been cast as the upstart nerd in an eighties teen movie, and pop him in the face like George McFly. (Important: It needs to be a *real* punch. If you have to pay the guy an extra few bucks, then so be it. Trust me, it's well worth it. For believability's sake.)

By the time the faculty breaks it up, you will have become a folk hero the likes of which that fucking school has never seen. And after you do your time in detention (the high-school version of "the hole"), you will emerge a mythical god. Your stooge will have "transferred," and you will rule the campus like a king, the newly printed protagonist in a present-day Horatio Alger story.

GET THE VICE PRINCIPAL FIRED

There are certain basic truths in this world, facts about this life that cannot be debated or debunked: there are three hundred sixty-five days in a year, guys with tattoos that completely encircle their upper arms are always fucknuts, and all vice principals employed by the vast and varied public school systems inside the United States are insecure weasels that take out their frustrations regarding the failures in their own lives on tenth and eleventh graders. It doesn't help that the basic job description is "enforcing punishments on the entire student body," which makes them tantamount to a warden (again, another prison analogy—more on that later). And, just like in the penitentiary, the one thing more impressive you can do than taking down a shot caller is taking down the warden himself. This is the one that worked for me at Providence High West (not the school's real name).

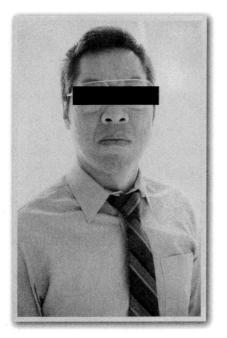

There are multiple ways to dispose of the most despised character on all school campuses: Murder (too messy). Get them transferred (too much work). Or you can use your head and do what I did to Vice Principal Wong (not his real name). Ruin the bastard's reputation, never to be rehabilitated. Therefore ending their reign as a VP of anywhere.

Now, there are a few ways to accomplish this goal. So you'll want to pick the one that'll be the most notorious as well as the most effective, something so big that he or she wouldn't be able to worm their way out of it. And subsequently back into your life, looking for revenge. It also needs to be something that you could clearly take credit for, something so amazing that it wouldn't just get him or her fired but, in fact, get them arrested. And that's exactly what happened with Vice Principal Wong.

Look at this asshole. The beady eyes and the get-off-my-lawn-glasses. I bet if he had ever *actually* met her, even his birth mother wouldn't have liked him. So after my first day at John Adams High School (not the real name), I knew that I hated him (as did the rest of the student body). In order to make a name for myself and get rid of this dildo, I decided to kill two birds with one stone. Not in a subtle way, but in the most spectacular way possible . . .

FIND YOUR MARK

Like I said earlier, this is *usually* the vice principal, because they tend to deal with punishments and suspensions. But depending on where you go to school, you could find your dupe in any and all sections of the faculty directory. And mind you, this is America! Assholes come in all shapes and sizes in the good ol' U.S. of A.

THE GYM TEACHER

Sociological studies show that 90 percent of all PE teachers are douche-nozzles. That is a quantified, empirical fact proven by modern science. They thrive on discovering just how much humiliation they can dish out in fifty-five-minute intervals, typically bestowed upon the weakest and most defenseless of the school (as if the bullies needed any help with that group). Whether he's shaming you in front of the popular girls for unsuccessfully attempting to climb a frigging rope, or forcing you to take a group shower with the older boys before your young body has had a chance to grow any considerable hair on your undercarriage, the gym teacher is that rare animal that redirects his anger at God (about having to wear coach's shorts to work and maxing out at $31K a year) and unloads that shit right onto you.

THE HANDSOME PERV

I think we all remember this character, right? Early twenties. Partied so hard in college that all he could manage to attain by the time he graduated (short of genital herpes) was a crummy English lit degree. And even worse, he looks like he could *still* be a student. In fact, sometimes he forgets that he isn't. If you're a dude and you're unlucky enough to be in this jagoff's class, you're fucked. Count on straight Cs because you don't have double Ds. All the male students hate this jerk because he's a total poser. And all the girls think he's dreamy because he always writes a new motivational haiku every morning on his dry-erase board and drives a convertible Smart car (having no idea they'll soon be judging prospective male mates by the size of their 401(k)s and not by how rad their faux-hawk looks). Getting rid of this fuckwit will get you celebrated by 50 percent of the student body, minus the gay kids in drama class. (By Federal Law, there's *always* at least two gay kids in drama class.)

THE LATINO SECURITY GUARD

I know what you're saying: "Why does he have to be Latino?" Well, he doesn't. He can also be black. Either way, no matter what race he is, this dude is always super annoying—telling you to pick up trash or to stop smoking butts in the bathroom. He's usually a thirty-something degenerate who loots marijuana from your locker because he has a master key. He's typically a graduate of the school and almost always a former athlete who incessantly talks about his inflated forty-yard-dash times and how he used to be *runnin' thangs* back in the day. This guy is most definitely a galactic toolbox. If you can get *him* fired, it would certainly be a notch on your likability belt. Now, back to Vice Principal Wong . . .

In case you already forgot, this guy was a supremely unlikable soul. And while what I did to him may seem cruel and unusual, even the United States Supreme Court would rule that this prick had it coming. Let me tell you that this was the same Vice Principal Wong who had prom canceled because there had been too much "bumping and grinding" going on the year before (his quote). The same Vice Principal Wong who made all the guys tuck in their shirttails because "this is a high school, not some flippin' disco-dance club" (also verbatim). Like I said, he had it coming. Why Principal Kelley gave him so much unchecked power, I didn't understand at the time.

So now that you've chosen your **mark**, like my Vice Principal Wong, let me explain how to get rid of him or her. Once again, please keep in mind that these lessons I'm teaching you to utilize in a school setting also translate to your regular, everyday adult life (work, the PTA, etc.).

Now, before anything else, you need to find their weakness. Which could be any number of things. For some, it's hiding a fifth of Seagram's Seven in their morning thermos. For others, it's hiding babysitter porn on their work hard drive in a file marked "Joel Osteen Quotes." Maybe it's a skeleton in their closet—like a hidden Dominican love child or a very recently expunged manslaughter rap. But as soon as you find that *thing*, that *Achilles' heel*, it is your duty to exploit it. And in Mr. Wong's case, it was obviously Nurse Sanchez.

Each day, I studied Vice Principal Wong, looking for any kind of susceptibility. I watched him eat his lunch. I followed him home to observe him interacting with his terrible family who clearly hated him. (And rightly so, the poor bastards.) I even sat in the stall next to him every single time he dropped a deuce. (You need to be dedicated, folks.) And after all that, I found nothing. Nothing, that is, until I noticed one little thing—one tiny anomaly in the monotonous algorithm that was his horrible excuse for a life. He got headaches. And I don't mean sometimes. I mean this dude got headaches every other fucking day, and they always seemed to hit him around the same time. You could set your watch by them. Initially, this didn't strike me as odd. But people are creatures of habit. Specifically, *bad* habits. And if you can pinpoint those patterns, then you've *got 'em cold.*

Ordinarily, there are only two reasons that you visit the school nurse every Tuesday and Thursday for a month because of chronic headaches: (1) you have an inoperable brain tumor with only months to live, or (2) said nurse is crazy fucking hot.

And for that reason I set up a **sting** (a complicated confidence game planned and executed with great care). The next time Mr. Wong got one of his "debilitating migraines," I followed him into the nurse's office, figuring I'd catch him with our school nurse in a very compromising position. (Hopefully sexual in nature.) But as it turns out, I was wrong. He wasn't with Ms. Sanchez every Tuesday and Thursday at 12:35 p.m. The nurse was actually at lunch at that time. No, he was with Principal Kelley. And since this was a school in the backward-ass Bible Belt and less empathetic toward this type of lifestyle—you know, because Jesus and everything—I had him.

If the guy hadn't been a total dickhead, I would have felt bad. But he was. So I didn't. And two hundred photocopies later, I was becoming an even bigger player on campus. Hooray for me!

Another way to get your name out there is . . .

BECOME CLASS PRESIDENT

This one is a bit more problematic, as these elections don't have much to do with platforms or policy; technically they're little more than popularity contests (you know, like real presidential elections). And being the new kid, there's practically no way you're going to win without cheating (as if any politician has ever won anything without cheating). So, a few helpful hints include:

STUFF THE BALLOT BOX

Teachers are always looking for suck-up kids to help them do the grunt work on shit like this, from putting up posters and setting up voting booths to collecting the votes from each classroom. This last one is vital. But be sure to volunteer for all aspects of the election, so as to not look too fishy. (That's a rule for everything, too, like pretending to be interested in the ugly friend in order to get closer to the hot chick.) And then, on your way back to the Student Government room, you merely switch the box for one that holds some five hundred votes with your name on them.

THREATEN THE FRONT-RUNNER

I don't mean to a healthy debate, either. I mean *literally* threaten them. Don't be overly dramatic or verbose when doing this. Go with something straightforward and to the point, like, I don't know, "If you win this election I will kill all of the members of your family who live at 3446 Sandburn Drive where you leave an extra key under the back doormat." This type of thing'll usually do the trick.

PAY OFF THE SOCIAL STUDIES TEACHER

In the 1990s, when I was in high school, the head of the Econ department made about $24K (I think that translates to a whopping $32K in today's money). And to add insult to injury, he was charged with the task of overseeing this sham replication of the Democratic process. Much like the UN, these teachers have very little interest in witnessing free and fair elections. And much like the UN, they can easily be bought off. My dad used to say, "To a dirty dog, all people are equal. Except for those people holding treats." And the bastard was right.

ASSASSINATION

I don't recommend this option, but one can hardly argue with its effectiveness.

Another way of getting your name out there is . . .

THE HERMES EFFECT

Another guaranteed way to get popular fast on campus is to be an amazing athlete. There was only one problem with that option for me (and for the 99.9 percent of you mega nerds reading this book right now). I was *not* one. But that doesn't mean you can't have the *reputation* of being one. (You will soon realize, when it comes to success in life, an inflated reputation from past deeds is *far* more important than any present-day triumphs.)

Now, I'd bet right now you're probably feeling quite dubious about this notion. How on earth might somebody become a varsity athlete when they throw like a *Trans-Gen, Special Olympian*? Well, look at it this way: you're not creating a great athlete, per se. You're merely creating the *reputation* of a great athlete. Big difference.

Now, I know that in this day and age, this will be a bit more difficult. But sometimes *old* tactics just need *new* adjustments. Back in the early 1990s there was no such thing as the Internet, so when I came to St. Ignacious Preparatory Academy for Boys (not the real name), I enrolled under an assumed name: Ronald J. Westerfield. Who was Ronald J. Westerfield, you ask? Well, he was a straight-A student, an all-conference wrestler, and he used to live *way* on the other side of the country. (Also important: For this scam to work, you need to pick a sport that is out of season. If it's fall, you're an all-conference baseball player. If it's spring, you lettered three times in soccer. Get it?) And arriving at the start of the semester like I did, I was Ronnie J. Westerfield, Wyoming state champ at 163 pounds. And in those days all I needed were a few important items:

A braggy and obnoxious thrift-store letterman's jacket.

A doctored transcript that makes you physically ineligible to participate.

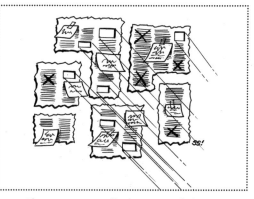

Phony newspaper clippings any asshole can doctor for you at Kinkos.

An arm cast. And add some fake signa-
tures to it. That's always a nice touch.

The last item is only necessary when you end up staying a little longer than you had anticipated, as I did at West Beach Polytechnic High School (nope). By the time wrestling season came around, I just slipped that baby on my arm, told my story about saving some old bat from some demented hobo on angel dust, and rode the bench in comfort and style. Admittedly in the present day, with social media being the bastion of bragging and bloviating that it is, this will be a little more challenging, but still doable. Firstly, you need to create a fake high school from which you transferred. "How does one fabricate a high school?" you say. Well, *you* don't. You hire a Pakistani kid from Geek Squad (or any other compu-tech equivalent) to construct a phony school website for you. Where you are not only the wrestling champ and class president, but also the lead in *West Side Story* and a member of the National Honor Society. (Important note: Keep a computer nerd on the payroll. Recruit a genius techie with enough incentive, and they can pretty much hack you into the institution of your choosing.) Which brings us to our next chapter . . .

GET A DEGREE *VIA* DEGREES OF BULLSHITTING

After pseudo-graduating from high school, my ambition led me to pretend-matriculate at a prestigious college of my liking. Of course, if you just want a diploma to proudly display on your wall so your new girlfriend doesn't know you're actually a fucking idiot, there are at least three hundred sites on the Internet, right now, that can replicate a pretty decent one in less than ten minutes. All for around thirty bucks. But these are good for only the most rudimentary of scams, like if you gambled away your tuition for four years and have nothing to show your ignoramus parents. Or if you're applying for some low-level sales job that requires a four-year degree. (Low-level jobs never check up on that stuff. That's why they're "low-level" jobs.) However, if you were like me and you wanted to engage in the entirety of the collegiate experience (minus the studying and the learning and shit), there is another way.

You see, I wanted to expand my mind and broaden my horizons (and refine my art of **working the hustle** on the young and the very dumb). And since my old man was still locked up, I figured I had some time to kill before our inevitable reunion. So I picked a very prominent school by the name of Harvard College (not Harvard), and I decided to take the first step toward the next chapter of my life. Tops on my to-do list was, of course. . . getting accepted. And as I didn't officially exist, this was the fundamental problem I would have to resolve before I could set foot on the historic campus of Yale University (not Yale).

There are numerous ways to get accepted into college when you have no business doing so. First and foremost, you need to decide what your goals are. Do you want to get laid? Do you want to get a prestigious degree? Do you want to avoid the government (bail, draft, etc.)? *U.S. News & World Report* has lists for everything. Therefore, it's necessary to know *exactly* what you're looking to get out of your collegiate experience before you head down this road. You don't want to waste your precious time beating a system you have no real interest in getting anything out of.

As far as I was concerned, I was doing all of this to impress my dad. Prove something to the son of a bitch. Because wherever he was, I knew he would have been proud of me for what I was about to pull off. Not for getting into Cornell (not Cornell), which is an accomplishment in its own right. But rather, for getting into Cornell *without* having *any* of the prerequisite grades or accomplishments necessary for actual *acceptance* there. He would have been most proud of me for *NOT* belonging there. In fact, I think he would have gotten a kick out of that. And, as pissed as I was at him, I would have gotten a kick out of him enjoying it, too. Anyway, enough of the sentimental reminiscing. This isn't a book about self-realization or any of that hippy-dippy horseshit. Let's get back to how I did it.

One of the best and most often executed ways to start is to . . .

GET A FAKE IDENTITY

This is a quick go-to. Tons of students use fake IDs to forge their way into colleges every year across this great nation. And while this fact may piss off some of you college graduates out there, if you're being *really* honest with yourself, you know that the true assholes are those of you who busted your asses with SAT prep courses and ROTC classes and all that other pointless nonsense you did to stack your résumé. Because the truth is something you're too young to realize at the time: the whole thing is a charade and not nearly worth the time you invest in it. So to avoid all the effort of building a great college résumé, just have your payrolled computer whiz kid fabricate one to rival the best and brightest of American kids. And also every single Indian kid between the ages of eighteen and twenty-two. (Note: This next section is something that you can use in the future, even after you falsely graduate. So pay attention.)

BECOME A MISSING PERSON

2,300 missing persons are reported in the US every day. And one would assume that at the very least, a small percentage of those poor fuckers did pretty well in high school. Calm down—I can feel your judgmental glares raining down on this *supposedly* recycled paper as you read this. "How terrible! I could never do such a thing!" Let me ask you, then, what would you actually be doing that's so terrible anyway? When I stole his identity, James Bradford (not his real name) had been missing for four years. FOUR YEARS. The odds of him ever accepting the financial aid that was awarded to him in order to go to Brown (not the real school) were less than nil. As a result, while Jimmy was most likely face down in some shallow grave out in the middle of a cornfield somewhere, yours truly was using his name to snap a passport picture and take over where that unlucky bastard left off. (Note: If a college-age kid already has a passport picture, 95 percent of the time it will be of them as a child. Translation: you're all good in the "you don't look anything like Jimmy" department.) And think about it—*not* using the money would have been the real tragedy, if you ask me. So just like that, I was off to the races, ready to fulfill some other person's unfulfilled destiny, headed straight for the hallowed halls of Cornell (nope).

But if you *still* find this practice too distasteful to engage in, (1) you're a total pussy, and (2) there are other methods to use.

BUY AN IDENTITY

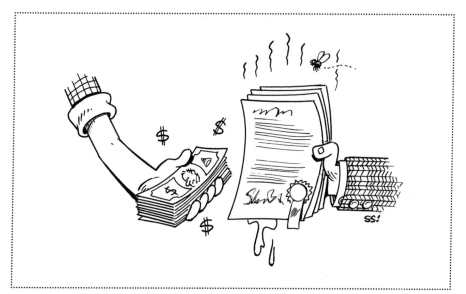

Ten million dumbasses get their identities stolen every year. And that shit doesn't just happen by osmosis. Somebody is making money off the hustle. Somebody is *always* making money off the hustle. Because if there's a need, consequently, there will be a black market to meet that need (see the failed "war on drugs"). Anyway, that's where you come in. First thing on the agenda: you have to hang out by the border. Any border. Texas. Arizona. Hell, even Niagara Falls, if you can believe it. Troll a few bus stops and train stations and you're bound to run into somebody who will sell you a birth certificate and an accompanying Social Security number, Patriot Act be damned. And people often use this information for buying cars, procuring home loans, getting jobs, and, in your case, applying to get into Duke (uhn-uhn).

FABRICATE YOUR ACCOMPLISHMENTS

Let's assume that you want to get into an Ivy League school. You'll need to have a pretty impressive academic record. This means top SAT scores, straight A's on your transcripts, and a slew of obnoxious extracurricular activities to set you apart from the rest of the multitude of dorks looking to fill your spot. Unfortunately, as it turns out, being an overachiever is a total pain in the ass. So when it does come to the "achievements" part of the application, you're gonna really have to go balls deep.

Now, you're probably asking yourself three things, "Won't they verify the information in my application to make sure that it's accurate? What if I get in trouble for falsifying official documents? Why did God make me such a gigantic pussy?"

Would you please quit your whining already? The dirty little secret universities don't want you to know, the reason students are able to fake their way into esteemed colleges all across the country each year: admissions officers don't have the time nor the inclination to scrutinize every single applicant as closely as they should. Because, as a wise woman said recently on the news, "Ain't nobody got time for that."

Generally speaking, most universities have tens of thousands of undergraduate applications to screen every semester. TENS OF THOUSANDS. And there's just not enough manpower or resources to verify that all of the information provided is authentic. So, unfortunately—or fortunately, depending on how you look at it— most universities rely on the "honor system" (ha ha ha). And since most admissions officers are gullible, apathetic, and/or both, they generally take you at your word more often than not. Which is exactly what the university gets for paying some working stiff well under forty Gs to be the gatekeeper of their self-righteous institution of higher learning (an institution with endowments generally north of twenty billion, by the way—think on that shit for a hot second when you think the system ain't rigged).

Here's the analogy: when you toss some poor valet the *keys to the kingdom*, without paying him a wage relative to a decent standard of living, don't be surprised when Pedro drives your shit right into a wall and hightails it for the border.

BLEND IN

After you get accepted, the next step is to not stick out like the dumbass that you actually are. Nothing can ruin your day more than the FBI showing up in the middle of your Intro to Stats class holding a warrant for your arrest. And believe it or not, getting in is the easy part. *Staying* in is where it becomes more difficult. Eventually, nearly all the students who fake their way into college get caught, and commonly, the reason they get caught is because they've failed to integrate into their environment well enough. Dissolving, unnoticed, into the sea of student humanity. And there's a good reason for that. Most of these kids actually deserve to be there. Fucking dorks. So, there are a lot of ways you can screw up, such as . . .

GETTING GREEDY

Look, I'm all for milking a moment. But there's something in *The Game* we call **gilding the lily**. That means when you're deep into a scam, you can sometimes forget that the world you're in isn't the *real* world. Your life becomes so normal inside of the lie that you forget it's a lie to begin with. And you start to unknowingly perpetrate

FULLBRIGHT SCHOLARSHIP to the COLLEGE of your CHOICE BUNDLES O' CAH$!!!
FOR:

scams inside the scam. This is a big no-no and something for which you should be on high alert.

For example, if you've made it into Stanford by hook and by crook (more crook), you need to keep a low profile. The last thing you need to do is to draw attention to yourself by trying to get the president emeritus's endorsement for the Rhodes Scholarship or by starting Stanford's very first Yurok Indian Service Fraternity. *Gilding the lily* is a huge red flag to the powers that be. The school will then be forced to take a closer look at your background and credentials, which we've already established to be total horseshit, and this will inevitably lead to you getting pinched.

NOT ACTING LIKE A STUDENT

If you're a grifter, there is nothing worse for business than *looking* like a grifter. If you're in college, and all of your dorm mates are always studying, while you've never had the good sense to, at the very least, carry around a bunch of books, then you *should* get pinched. Because you, sir, are a dumbfuck. Just buy a backpack, for chrissakes. Fill it with books, or dirty laundry, or cinder blocks for all I care. Then head out to the library, put a titty mag inside some boring text about French Impressionism, and just . . . play the part. It's not that difficult. But little mistakes, like not knowing when spring break is, are **scammer colds** that can quickly develop into **full-blown hustle fevers**. And as we all know, fevers can kill you.

BECOME A TA

This is what I did. As soon as I got into Princeton (which was not where I went), I found the softest mark (refer to earlier chapter) and looked for vulnerabilities therein. Again, weak spots. You see, a lot of people just choose a major, and then get assigned a professor. Not me—instead I sat in forty-some classes looking for the frailest professor I could find, and *then* I let that major choose me. (Note: Remember what I said earlier about reverse engineering your life. It is the only guaranteed path to success. If you know where you're going to end up, then you know exactly where to begin.)

His name was Dr. Edgar Heatherford (that's pretty close, actually), and he had been at the university for going on seven hundred fifty years. He was what they call "long tenured," or what we call in the business "fucking vulnerable." There is nothing better than a smart person who is losing his faculties. Not for him, I mean. For him, it must suck nuts. I meant for me. The con man. The guy who is going to roll him. Good stuff. Anyway, it didn't take long for me to become close with Edgar. "James, you remind me of myself when I was your age," he'd tell me.

"Well, thank you, sir. I could only hope to be as accomplished as you someday," I'd reply in an English accent (a nice touch, I thought) as I was stealing the exams from his briefcase and selling them to anybody with two hundred dollars and a C-minus average or lower.

Dr. Heatherford was a nice old man. He cared about me. He really wanted good things for his star pupil, James Bradford, or "Jimmy Boy," as he sometimes liked to call me (having no idea that the real Jimmy Boy was probably at the bottom of a lake somewhere with a boulder tied around his Nikes).

"I really like you. You're going places, son." You're goddamned right I am, Doc. You have no idea.

That old prick never had a chance. Pay attention here, because this is a *teachable moment*. In order to get ahead in life, certain words should be verboten from your own personal vocabulary. Words like *empathy* and *compassion*, or the worst of them all, *pity*. Ugh, *pity*. Look, did I feel bad that the once-brilliant Dr. Heatherford was becoming increasingly maladroit? Sure. Since the day my dad bailed on me, Dr. Heatherford was the closest thing I'd had to a father figure. Shit, I really liked the old guy. He was generous. And kind. And being around him so much actually made me miss my old man.

But did I feel the least bit guilty that I was taking advantage of his elderly naiveté? **No, I did not.** And why is that? Because it was his own fault. He didn't know when to quit. When to call it a career. Like the incredible Michael Jordan, pushing forty years old, averaging a pedestrian (for him) 19 points, 6 rebounds, and 3 assists a game with the Washington Wizards. That shame was on him. Not the younger guy humiliatingly shutting him down on D in front of 18,000.

One day, I thought, when I'm off my game for one reason or another, and I get apprehended on some stupid rudimentary setup because I can no longer "stay in the zone" like I used to be able to, do you know who I'll have to blame for that? Me. In fact, part of me would be relieved by it. Impressed, even. And that is because the laws of Darwin are applicable not only to evolution, but to *all* human interaction. Only the strong survive. Survival of the fittest. Outwit, outlast, outplay. (That last one I got from *Survivor*, but you get the idea.) Did I like the old fart? Of course I did. Did it keep me from swindling his ass? Not a Slurpee's chance in hellfire. I took every class he taught. In fact, I took *only* the classes he taught. And when you know the answers to all the tests beforehand, you tend to do pretty damn well. And I did. Appreciate you, Dr. H! Heaven eventually gained one really smart angel, I'm guessing.

FINDING YOURSELF BY DEFRAUDING OTHERS

Aside from getting a phony degree and stealing the dignity of a once-proud old man, I used college as a practice ground for my craft. (Looking back on it now, I see that each and every one of these experiences was leading me to my supreme scam. And the hustle that would change my life forever. But more on that later.) Young people go to college because they are unfit to live and work in the real world. They are something I call **middlers**, floating aimlessly in that soft spot between youth and adulthood. They're the perfect unsuspecting group on which a guy can hone his skill set, this giant phylum of inexperienced dummies still suckling at Mommy and Daddy's teat, ready and willing to be taken advantage of. And that's exactly what I did. I went to college to increase my aptitude in that respect. That's what you're supposed to do there anyway, right? I just worked on a more practical skill set is all.

Anyhow, in most of the boring con men books you come across, they spend the entire however-many-pages showing you the basics, teaching you all the cons that have been done for centuries on end, each con getting its own chapter. I find that to be a bit too rudimentary for my liking. Instead, I will use these next few pages to quickly run you through them all. During my go-round in college, instead of working on Spanish, I was working the **Spanish prisoner** (see below). Instead of studying, I was **stacking** (prearranging playing cards so that you always get the best hand). And instead of finishing, I was **phishing** (convincing people to give up their personal information and then, in turn, using that information to fleece them).

So here's a list of some of the classics. I'll try not to bore you with too many details. As I said earlier, the simpler you keep the grift, the higher the chance you'll have of succeeding with it.

THE EMBARRASSING CHECK

The embarrassing check con is a well-known means of legally getting money from men by playing off their innate feelings of shame and self-hatred. The con man first opens up a *legitimate* business with an overtly explicit company title. Opening an LLC (limited liability company) nowadays is fairly easy to do.

Then you toss out some lures. Tell the buyers that any purchases they make from your questionable business will be routed through a separate company with a much more innocuous name.

After taking orders and collecting payments, the company (that's you) then sends the perverted asshole a letter explaining that a shipping error or some other bullshit issue has made it impossible for them to deliver their product. You then enclose a *legitimate* check refund—only this time the highly graphic name of the company is clearly emblazoned on the check.

The idea, of course, is that a very high percentage of the customers of said filth will be too ashamed to ever cash that check. Boom. Easy money.

THE PIG IN A POKE

This is one of the oldest cons in the book. My old man taught it to me when I was, like, four. ("A child's brain is like a sponge, so soak alla this up, dipshit," he'd often muse.) I think it dates back to medieval times or something. Anyway, back when there wasn't a McDonald's on every corner and beef *wasn't* highly subsidized for absolutely no reason except to grease fast-food corporations and starve the entire continent of Africa, meat was scarce, and pigs and cows were often *rightly* worth large sums of money. So, in this particular con, the trickster offers to sell another person a baby pig. (I know, it's weird, but just go with this for a second.)

After receiving the money, they would hand over a "poke," or burlap sack, that clearly had a squirming live animal in it.

If the sucker neglected to check inside the bag, which they oftentimes did in those days, they would be surprised when they arrived home to find that the sack contained a different form of meat.

The term "buying a pig in a poke" has since become a common expression referring to making a risky purchase under very questionable circumstances. Even the phrase "let the cat out of the bag" dates back to this well-known con. (Note: The present-day version of this con is when some unsuspecting, greedy fool buys "studio-quality speakers" from the back of some Hispanic illegal's van in a crowded Vons parking lot.)

THE BADGER GAME

This is arguably one of the most reproduced gimmicks of all time. The most famous version is the following: A con woman seeks out some lonely married man at a bar. (Horny guys are often made lightheaded and irrational from all the blood rushing from their brains down to their junkbag.)

She then approaches the guy, lets him buy her a drink, and starts up your average flirtatious conversation this loser would never normally attract.

She then lures this disgusting slob back to her hotel room and immediately gets him into some compromising position he'd be more than happy to assume.

She takes some pictures of the dumb prick and threatens to email them to his wife, place of business, church rectory, etc. That is, unless he pays up. And does so in cash.

It's often smart for the woman to work in tandem with a male **coadjutor** (a second grifter back-up) who shows up in the middle of things and pretends to be "the angry husband" or "the undercover vice cop"—which almost always helps to scare the mark into going along with the blackmail. Like the embarrassing check scheme, the idea is that the victim would be too ashamed of his own actions *not* to pay off the con men, and if you add a coadjutor, also fearful that he might get his fucking ass kicked. (Lesson here, boys: If you look like a troll from Middle Earth, always be skeptical of an attractive woman with two functioning eyeballs trying to get you back to her room in order to perform fellatio on you.)

THE SPANISH PRISONER

Have you ever gotten one of those junk emails from a fella with a first name like "Agbapuonwu" telling you that you just won the Nigerian Lotto? Of course you have. You live on planet Earth. So then, you're familiar with the "Spanish prisoner," which is what we in the Game call the ***advance-fee fraud***. The angle is to fool unsuspecting marks by promising them a big payday down the road with only a little cash upfront. Seems totally reasonable, right?

Apparently this scam dates all the way back to the late 1500s, when it was often used against wealthy businessmen, not regular schmucks like you. This is how it would go down: After gaining his mark's trust, a con man would intimate that he was corresponding with the family of a fabulously wealthy person of high social class (think some olden-time Kardashians)—a *noble* who was being imprisoned in Spain for a crime they didn't commit. Why Spain, I have no idea, but go with it.

Fearing some sort of scandal, the prisoner has not yet released his name or the details of his case to the public, and is relying on private means to generate the money to secure his release.

With this in mind, the mark would be told that any money he contributed to help the cause would be paid back with interest when it's all over. In some variations, it would even be implied that the person would get to marry the Spanish prisoner's

beautiful daughter. (Remember, this is some olden-days shit. When that kinda stuff really happened.)

Naturally, any money the victim gave upfront would inevitably disappear, and when possible, the con man would even try to get his victim to contribute more and more cash by telling them that a rescue attempt or another high-level payoff needed to be funded. (In my opinion, if you *do* send money a second time, it's best to just go put on some dark clothing at night and run headfirst into heavy traffic.)

THE PONZI SCHEME

Back when I was pretending to be in college, this was referred to as a **pyramid scheme**. If current events (and every episode of *American Greed*) have proven anything, it is that there is no more potentially profitable hustle than the good old Ponzi scheme. This trick dates back a hundred years and was popularized by a clever fella by the name of Charles Ponzi, an Italian immigrant to the US who swindled investors out of millions in the early 1900s before finally being arrested. Which is pretty amazing, when you think about it, because the Italians were basically the Mexicans of those days.

The modern Ponzi scheme is a form of investment fraud in which a corrupt stock-broker uses the cash of his new investors to pay the imaginary returns of his old ones.

The initial investments with the fictitious broker always yield enormous returns for the greedy morons being conned, but in reality their money hasn't been invested in shit. The ripper has simply been putting it all into his own bank account. And when someone wants to withdraw money, or if he has to pay the returns of his old investors, the con man simply uses the money he's gotten from new investors to do so. It's just that easy.

Nothing is ever invested, won, or lost in the market. The con man is merely giving that impression so imbeciles keep handing over more and more cash. (Guaranteed returns are always a telltale sign of chicanery, by the way, so look out, dummies.) Now, because the money can only grow so far, all Ponzi schemes are destined to eventually collapse under their own weight. As a result, the con man usually skips town after gathering enough cash to do so comfortably, leaving the investors with nothing but forged returns in one hand and their penises in the other.

(Note: Charles Ponzi indeed tried to flee America on a merchant ship but was arrested in New Orleans, served ten years in prison, and died penniless. And, as my father would always tell me, "A true American pioneer whose birthday should be celebrated like Washington and Lincoln and all those other phonies they build pointless statues for. Remember that, dipshit.")

I'd bet even ol' Chuckie P. would be shocked at how far people have taken his ingenious innovation just one hundred years later. As you probably well know (unless you've been living under an overpass selling fake Gucci handbags), another American vanguard, Bernard Lawrence Madoff, engineered a Ponzi scheme estimated to be in the neighborhood of $65 billion. That's billion with a b, folks. Madoff was eventually caught and sentenced to one hundred fifty years in prison, but not before pulling off what was essentially the biggest con of all time.

That is, until I would eventually come up with something even more artistic, if not lucrative. A scam so big and intricate and innovative that even Pops would end up being proud of me. An ANGLE that would have ANGLES inside of ANGLES! But we'll get to that a little later; for now, let's talk about you . . .

MAKING IT IN THE REAL WORLD BY BEING *REALLY* FAKE

After I "graduated" from college with a four-year degree, I got an "MBA" for shits and giggles. (I've always been a bit of an overachiever in that way.) And then, like most college grads, I moved to the Big City to officially start my career. I had given up on the idea of ever reconnecting with my father again. Furthermore, I had come to the reasonable conclusion that I would probably never see him alive again. And I was okay with that. Todd Peterson (no way) was officially on his own now. And he was going to make a fake name for himself, no matter what it took. And not only was I going to make my absentee father proud, but I was going to surpass all of his exploits, too. If for nothing less than to shit on his memory.

By the way, in my line of work, only dimwits and rookies use their actual birth names. It's kinda like being a truck stop stripper. The more awful the titty bar, the more awful the fake names the girls inevitably have. They choose what they believe to be "sexier" aliases. Real bullshitty ones like "Elegance" or "Delicious." Well, in my business, we do the exact opposite. We shoot for dull. We prefer plain. Purposely choosing the least sexy name possible for each and every new **rip**. Because most folks like to hear a nice, generic introduction coming from a stranger's mouth. "Hi there, my name is Mahmoud Behrooz al-Rahim. Would you mind watching my oversized backpack for a moment?" That kinda thing doesn't usually go over very well in present-day America.

Don't overthink it either—nothing too clever or exotic. Nothing to turn a person's defenses on. Mundane equals comfortable, and comfortable equals vulnerable, and vulnerable is the gold fucking standard. That's why something as vanilla and banal as "Todd Peterson" is ideal. Todd Peterson is a stiff nobody who pays his taxes early, fucks his wife an average of three times annually, and never, ever throws his jury duty summons right in the trash.

For the record, I've been a Jerry, an Adam, and a Prince William. I've also been married, widowed, and divorced. I've been a doctor, a lawyer, and in every branch of law enforcement (where I served honorably and with distinction, by the way). I can speak in all regional dialects. I have been a card-carrying member of all political parties and affiliations, left, right, and center. And I've been pretty much every nationality I could pull off without having to wear makeup or a dot on my forehead.

As you may or may not know, living in the Big City is expensive, but there are some easy methods to reduce your expenses (food, shelter, and the like). I've detailed below how to acquire all the must-haves you will need going into this next phase of your life, like . . .

FOOD

There is real power in being able to enjoy a good meal at any time of the day. You don't believe me? Go spend a summer in western Africa. Seriously, next to fresh air, clean water, and free Wi-Fi, food is the main ingredient to sustaining life on Earth. And always being able to eat for free, anywhere, anytime—now *that's* true freedom. So as soon as you get off that long-ass bus ride from Nowhere, USA, make your way to the closest army-navy store, where for about twenty bucks, you can buy the following items:

The army fatigues of a dead person.	The Purple Heart of some one-legged asshole.	A sympathy inducing cane, as the handicapped cherry on top.

Circling back to *guilt*. As my father once told me, when I was around nine or so, "Guilt is like an STD. Everybody's had some, in one form or another. Especially whores. Remember that one, dipshit." And to his credit, it's at the emotional core of all good scams (see embarrassing check scam), because humans hate to feel bad about themselves. (Personal shame is the ultimate repellant.) They'd prefer to think of themselves as "good people," whatever the hell that means. (I've never actually had that particular affliction, thank goodness.) It's why you buy your kid an Xbox because you have zero interest in throwing the fucking baseball around with him after getting home from your terrible job at the who-gives-a-shit factory. It's why you put fifty bucks in the collection plate at your church right after you just finished having unprotected sexual intercourse with your teenaged Peruvian nanny. *Guilt.*

There is no greater guilt than the guilt regarding those who "protect and serve" us. (Remember this when you want to buy a coach ticket and then fly first class.)

"Thank you for your service," my ballsack. You're just psyched you didn't have to go *over there* and fight for your own goddamned freedoms instead of some poor sonovabitch who grew up in a terrible low-income, low-information household. A free meal??? Hell, the government should be giving these guys free blowjobs for life when they get back from whatever dusty turdbox they were just busy "liberating." But hey, don't get me going on the government. Next to organized religion, it's the biggest fucking racket going. Always has been. Another option for free food is . . .

THE RAT PACK

Things you'll need:

A sports coat that gives the illusion you could actually pay for the soup.	A pad of paper and pen that makes you look like an annoying busybody.	Actual rat droppings (don't cheat, be authentic!).

This is an oldie but a goldie. And it has nothing to do with Dean Martin or Frank Sinatra or that other drunk who married the forgettable Kennedy. Such an incredibly easy hustle to pull off—it's amazing everybody doesn't carry a bag of rat shit in their pocket at all times. Remember to dress in your Sunday best. Bring a pad and pen, like you're taking notes on the meal. Always order whatever the house specialties are, and make sure it's more than you could eat in one sitting, (1) to make it look like you're trying everything for a reason, and (2) because you won't be finishing any of them. Then, somewhere midmeal, you whisper to the waiter (asking him not to tell the owner, of course—which he most assuredly always will) that you're a food critic from a small local paper. (Don't be a dumbshit and say the *New York Times*. Restaurants keep tabs on stuff like that. Keep it simple, dipshit! Remember what Pops said?!) And be sure to tell the waiter, between you and him . . . that you've been very impressed, so far. Side note: Another rule of scamming people is that just as you can prey on their *guilt*, you can also prey on their *pride*. (The Seven Deadlies are a bitch, ain't they?)

Now, when you're almost full, you pull out your handy bag of rodent fecal remnants. Toss a few pellets in the soup (make sure to order the soup du jour). And when the owner comes out to greet you (and they always do), you gag on the stuff. Right in front of him or her. Side note: If you don't have mouse poop handy, this bit also works with a good pair of scissors and your pubes. Either way . . .

Your meal. Is now. Free.

THE PLUS ONE
Things you'll need:

A used tuxedo from some idiot who actually once purchased a fucking tuxedo.

Go to any thrift store and find yourself a vintage tuxedo. You'll have to pay a few bucks for the thing. But what you'll get back in gourmet meals will cover that twenty times over.

This particular scam is what I call a **weekender**, only to be executed during the non–workweek. (Co-opting the collection plate from church and embezzling cash gifts from a small child's birthday party are also **weekenders**.) If you live in a metropolis, there are approximately two thousand moronic weddings every weekend. That's right. Two. Fucking. Thousand. (Half of which will have ended in divorce by the same time next year, but that's a whole other book.) Go find one. And eat up while you can.

Next we have shelter . . .

RENT OUT A HOUSE YOU DON'T OWN

Even con men are subject to market conditions and need to play the hand they're dealt. So when the housing market inevitably crashes again as it did in 2008, two amazing things will happen. There will be a lot less terrible fucking *Flip-Flop* shows on HGTV. And also, thousands of abandoned homes will sit empty once more, leaving a multitude of people in need of cheap housing. Which means someone is eventually going to put the two together. So why not let it be you?

First on the agenda, find yourself an abandoned property or two. (Even in these days of the "economic recovery," it's really not that hard. See the housing market in non–Las Vegas, Nevada. And all of greater Detroit.) Then create an online advertisement pretending to be either the owner or someone authorized to rent on the owner's behalf. "Hi, I'm JoeBlow Bullshit from Somebody's a Total Moron Realty. How may I help you?"

Next, break into the house, change the front lock, and start seeing potential renters. Provide a contract along with a handwritten rental receipt (copies of these can easily be found online) and inform the **sucker** that the rent is to be paid in CASH only and he or she will have to meet you each month in a public location to collect payment. That way, if he or she tries to revenge-kill you, you'll have witnesses to your own murder.

And don't go feeling bad for your new tenants, you pussy. They didn't intend to occupy a house illegally and aren't going to be charged with a crime or anything. But they are going to have to move on short notice and are unlikely to see their security deposits again, mainly because they'll be in your pocket. And you'll already be on to the next house in a different city. Clever shit, right? I know.

DON'T PAY RENT

We all know, from watching way too much TV, that possession is nine-tenths of the law, so really all you need to do is falsify your identity when you turn in your rental application (see earlier). And then, once you get the keys to your new place, just don't pay. That's it. That's the entire hustle. Just. Don't. Pay. With the way our dysfunctional government works, it takes about a full year for somebody to legally get you the hell out of the dwelling. Other than that, the best they can do is wait you out. And because you're doing this on purpose, this is a stare-down they're bound to lose.

The only valid recourse they have is to ruin your credit. But since you're not the person they think you are, there's really no worry about any of that nonsense, now is there? Oh, and make sure to pick a building with a high volume of residents. The bureaucracy moves even slower in these places.

BECOME A DOCTOR BY DOCTORING YOUR MEDICAL BOARDS

R emember when you were little and grownups would tell you that you could be anything you wanted to be if you just put your mind to it? And then, do you remember the moment when life kicked you directly between both of your nuts and said, "You don't actually get to be an astronaut with a D+ average, Alan"? It's a big, fat lie told to every kid growing up so they don't eventually plot to overthrow the government or go on a shooting spree at their local Olive Garden. The fact that anybody remotely believes it in the first place is the real joke, child or not. Let's be honest, if you're born with achondroplastic dwarfism, there's no way in hell that you're gonna ever play power forward for the Knicks.

And conversely, there's zero shot that if you're born black, you could end up as president of the United States.

Okay, that one is admittedly an outlier. But for what it's worth, a majority of the residents of Hickistan don't think that he *actually* is. (See the earlier section on fake identities and forged birth certificates.)

Anyway, I am here to tell you that while the notion of being whoever you want to be is indeed the *ultimate* con perpetrated on all of humanity, if you follow the instructions of this book, in certain circumstances you *can* be anything you want to be, if temporarily. Like, say . . .

A DOCTOR

I can again imagine the gasps of disgust coming from those of you reading this particular section. Yeah, well, suck on it. Read the title on the cover again—it's a book about cheating at life. I'm not suggesting you become a cardiologist or brain surgeon or anything; I'm talking about becoming one of the shittier, less impressive types of doctors. You know, the ones that charge you $1,500 a pop for checking your blood pressure and putting an index finger inside your butthole. If you want to become one of these C-level-type physicians, you can either waste the entirety of your youth reading a thousand mind-numbing books about glands and viruses and the like, or you can just make believe that you already are one.

I don't know about you, but of all the times I've been to a doctor's office, I've never once checked his or her credentials. I've never checked their grades or their boards. Or where they ranked in their med school graduating class. Aside from quickly glancing at their wall of degrees and licenses, I never once thought to vet the person who was in charge of me *not* dying. This is another very important life lesson: people don't *really* want to fucking know. Their lives are already hard enough as it is. The last thing they need to worry about is what their general practitioner's undergraduate GPA at state college was.

Things you will need for this scam:

A stethoscope to hang around your neck pointlessly.

A white lab coat that makes you look like you've spent the morning "reading charts."

A framed medical license from any non-Ivy university.
You're an idiot, remember? So, don't overdo it.

After obtaining these items, go to a place where they need volunteers. A place where they can't be too picky about who shows up to help. Like a third-world country. Or a struggling senior center. Or Cleveland. Somewhere they'll be happy just to have you there, even if you flunked out of high school and the only state-run board exam that you passed had the letters G, E, and D in it. Most likely you'll only be taking people's pulses, looking down their throats, and prescribing antibiotics. (That's all most doctors really do 95 percent of the time anyway.) Make friends with some of the other volunteer doctors. (Generally speaking, they're do-gooder types, who are always the most trusting and naive.) Then use those connections to help you join a local practice, and similar to any other line of work—just learn on the job. It's kinda like working at Subway.

"The phony doctor will see you now, shithead."

A PILOT

If 9/11 taught us anything, it's that (1) our own government planned it (Hello, *obvs!*), and (2) any highly motivated inbred, *religified* lunatic can learn how to fly a fucking plane. It's actually a lot easier than one would think. The whole "ten thousand flying hours" is total horseshit in this case. If you want to be a pilot, and more importantly, fly for free all over the world, in business class no less, all you really need is the following:

A pilot's uniform. A discreet one.
Don't try looking like a Blue Angel.

A forged FAA license. Again, the Internet
is a dangerous place.

Twenty hours in a flight simulator. Just for fun, mostly.

These days, planes basically fly themselves. You just need to know the basics, and that's only if you are called on in an emergency to actually fly the plane. Which you *never* will be. You'll be too busy joining the mile-high club with some hot stewardess based out of Houston (if you're as lucky as I was).

A LAWYER

This is a no-brainer. There are so many lawyers out there nobody gives two shits to check if you're legit or not. I mean, who would pretend to be a lawyer, anyway? That would be like impersonating a known child molester or boasting at a Tea Party convention that you're starting your own ISIS splinter cell. Almost everybody on earth hates lawyers. They're the true soulless, unethical con men out there. Thus it's very easy to profess to be one. Things you will need for this con:

A suit that makes you look physically greasy.

An ad on the back of a bus in mostly Mexican neighborhoods.

A week's worth of law shows on TV, tops.

I'm aware that all the law shit you see on television usually consists of long, drawn-out cases where the attorneys use a very obscure vernacular, competing to see who can act more dramatic in some closing-argument showdown. But that actually resembles only some 2 percent of the cases that are filed in the United States of Lawsuits. If you want to make money, *real* money, look for marks that were injured at their miserable jobs, then take their employers to the cleaners without ever having to get in front of an actual judge or jury. Here's what you do: First, find out exactly what happened. Send the company in question a threatening letter with your fancy letterhead (you'll need some of that, too). And then wait for the money to come pouring in. It really is as simple as that.

Trust me, I know from personal experience that these rackets work. Because I've tried them all. I was a doctor, a pilot, and a lawyer. I was also a priest, a federal agent, and a psychiatrist. I lived more lifetimes in my one life than a hundred people will ever live in theirs. I made money. I gained prestige. I scored with more hot women than anybody not named Wilt. But there was always something missing in my life. An emptiness. Maybe it was all the moving I did as a kid. Or not having my dad around. Ever. At all. And even though I was able to become a chameleon in each environment, I never truly felt at home anywhere. And I guess that's what I was longing for. What something was *drawing* me toward.

I'm sure you're thinking, well, we're more than halfway through the book, so this must be the part where I tell you I changed my ways, right? Quite the contrary. This is the part where I tell you how uninspired I was. That I had done it all and there was nothing left to conquer in *The Game*. I was honestly surfing the web looking for somewhere to retire. And not because of a newfound conscience or maturity . . . but rather from a general indifference. Then at that moment, that *exact moment*, a pop-up appeared on my computer screen. It read . . .

So much to do in Indiana!

Famed analytic psychologist Carl Jung defined **synchronicity** as: *the occurrence of two or more events that appear to be meaningfully related but are not actually related.* For instance, Lincoln and Kennedy being elected exactly one hundred years apart, assassinated by Southerners, and succeeded by men named Johnson. Or the fact that literally every single one of Hugh Hefner's hostages/girlfriends looks identical to the last. This *synchronicity* shit basically makes the case that there are actually such things as "meaningful coincidences." I'd never really bought into any of this kind of hippy-dippy stuff until a certain line in that particular ad jumped out at me . . .

So much to do in Indiana!

Can you even believe that in this day and age, such a place exists?! And if there *were* such a place, why would you advertise it to the entire fucking world? A world filled with degenerates and criminals and con men like me? It's the equivalent of putting your Social Security number on Facebook and then Friending a bunch of Nigerians. *#Dumb.*

This was it! This was my calling! This was the moment that I had trained my entire life for. So for the next half of this book, I will focus on what's called the **long con**. These are always the most difficult cons, but also the most rewarding. For a full year, I did my research on this miracle of a town, all the players there, and the power structure that runs Honest, Indiana. (*Obviously* not the real name of the city. I've changed the name to protect the innocent, and more importantly, the *guilty*— me.) Organizations big and small, from grade school to the White House, *always* have a power structure. There are the *important people* and then there's *everybody else*. And if you can crack that first part, whoever and whatever it may be—ingratiate yourself with the folks that make things tick—you too can be running things. Which was *precisely* what I planned to do.

Social media has changed *The Game* more than any other innovation out there. Ten years ago, I would have had to move to and stake out that turd of a town for a good six months or so. But these days, I did it all on a laptop (which I stole at my local Starbucks from some asshole writing a terrible movie script about bisexual zombies—super easy, too. You just need a white cup and a Sharpie).

I found out everything I could about that place, like . . .

How many goofy cops they had (eleven)

How many pathetic banks there were (two)

How many unfortunate minorities lived inside the city limits (one)

I know that last one sounds a *splash* racist, but it's a good sign in this particular situation. The fewer minorities and the more lily white and homogenous the population, the more foolishly trusting the people there inevitably are. They can't help it. It's part of their DNA. These dopey fuckers don't know any better. They think all the bad stuff happens "out there" to "those people," but not in Honest, Indiana. Shit, in that place, even the landscapers are Caucasian.

I got to know the important "movers and shakers" of the place, from the president of the Kiwanis Club to the newly elected mayor, who, believe it or not, was a total douche-nozzle.

What is he? Nine? This is the "elected leader" of this town? Can you imagine? He looks like a hillbilly Kim Jong Un. It was almost gonna be too easy. And like I told you earlier, I had already played out the end, before I ever *thought* about the beginning. So for me, there would be no surprises. Or so I thought.

As you'll come to see, *synchronicity*, as it turned out, can sometimes be quite the motherfucker.

PART 2:

VICTIMIZING PEOPLE ON THE MACRO LEVEL

HOW TO BE AMBITIOUS IN YOUR DEPRAVITY

Everything I had learned and experienced so far in my life was leading me to this moment. This one *grand opportunity* to stake my claim. To leave my mark. To give more to *The Game* than I took from it. (Okay, maybe that last one was a bit hyperbolic.) I was about to embark into uncharted territory. My own Apollo 11. My personal 1492 (sans the mass extinction of indigenous peoples). I was about to take an entire town for a ride. And, in the end, go for quite the ride myself. But I'm getting ahead of myself again, so let me first explain that . . .

A **long con** is exactly what it sounds like. It refers to a variety of scams which require more planning, preparation, and/or a longer window of interaction with your *mark* or *marks*. A longer span of time is needed to accomplish all this. The long con may also require a larger crew and/or a greater number of people involved. Unlike a **short con**, the long con requires time to slowly draw the *John* into your hustle. So, by definition, LCs are more of a pain in the beanbag—but they're worth it because they almost always result in larger payouts than your average SC does. Due to the high levels of difficulty in organizing and executing, LCs are for experts like me. But because you bought (or hopefully stole) this book, I'm going to walk you through the best, baddest, and *most surprising* long con ever attempted in the history of *The Game*.

Traditionally, the term *long con* has referred to an elaborate scam of one or more suckers that ends with an enormous payout, in which the victims unwittingly surrender their cash, homes, companies, even countries, in some cases (take a quick peek at US history if you don't believe that last one). Long cons play on two basic human frailties: greed and desperation. A few classic examples of traditional long cons:

THE WIRE SCAM

The central idea is the **grifter** convinces the **dupe** they have advance knowledge of the outcome of some race results before they reach the off-track betting sites (which the grifter has created). As seen in that old movie *The Sting*, this is accomplished by having a **roper** (the member of the crew that lures in the sucker) with the ability to briefly delay results coming from a race, game, fight, etc., allowing the grifter and the dupe to place a bet before the results are released. The dupe is allowed to win some small bets early before placing a significantly larger one that will, of course, lose.

THE BOILER ROOM

Boiler rooms are often set up in inexpensive office spaces, where armies of tele-marketers make high-pressure cold calls. While the stock they sell may be real (most likely an unknown microcap stock), the information these salespeople use to hype their product, like a pending patent or some blockbuster acquisition, is most definitely bullshit. (Remember the classic "they're just weeks away from FDA approval of Viagra for women" scam was a big one for a while.) The only purpose of the army of automatons doling out totally misleading "insider speculation" is to sell the stock and claim their commissions. They'll often tout stocks that trade on the Pink Sheets or the Over-The-Counter Bulletin Board, as both of those exchanges don't have to meet the minimum requirements to file with the SEC. I know, I know. You're too dumb to understand what the hell I just said, right? Then just Netflick that Ben Affleck movie *Boiler Room*. It's basically *that*, only with shittier acting.

THE SWEETHEART CON

Also known as a **lonely hearts scam** or **sweetheart swindle**, this is literally one of the oldest tricks in this book. The con artist gains the affection of the mark, uses that affection to gain access to their money, and then makes off with the loot, never to look back. It's as elementary as that. Now, there are always variations of this baby, but the basic premise is the same: the mark falls in love with somebody *way* out of their league and will do anything for the sexy swindler—and then the sexy swindler bleeds them dry like the fool that they are. Sometimes it's money, sometimes it's citizenship, sometimes it's identity, but the end result is always the same—some rube getting rolled like pizza dough by a person far too attractive to be interested in them in the first place. "Svetlana and I are so in love we decided to get a joint bank account." Well, Das Vidania, Svetlana! Enjoy that ugly asshole's money back in the Ukraine!

**THE PONZI SCHEME
(SEE EARLIER)**

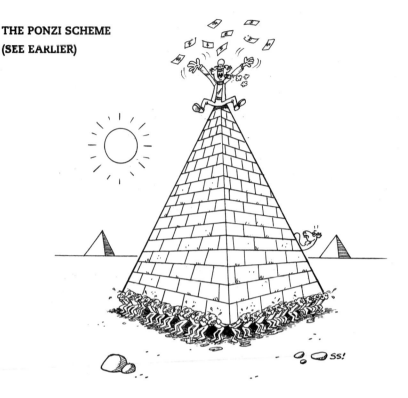

To reiterate for those of you with ADD, a Ponzi scheme is a sham investment operation where the operator, an individual or phony organization, pays "returns" to its investors from new capital paid to the operator by *new* investors, rather than from profits actually earned by the operator. The masterminds of Ponzi schemes usually entice new investors by offering higher returns than are mathematically possible or short-term returns that are abnormally high or unusually consistent. Basically, it's the old adage that if something sounds too good to be true, it *invariably* is.

But here's the thing: I'd done all of that mundane nonsense already. In fact, I'd mastered it all, to one degree or another. And I wasn't doing it for the money anymore. There's a reason the word *artist* is in the title of my chosen profession. Because this is more than just a vocation. It's a calling. Imagine if Jackie Robinson stayed in the Negro leagues for job security. Or if Abe Lincoln decided that being a representative from Illinois was good enough for him. (That's right, I'm comparing myself to President Abraham Lincoln. So what?) As far as I'm concerned, you should never, *ever* let "good enough" be good enough, especially in this business. (My old man taught me that one, too, along with how to steal all the UNICEF tins from every 7-Eleven in our neighborhood.) So let's get right to it. This is how you're going to scam an entire town . . .

MAKING A GOOD FIRST IMPRESSION
WHEN YOU'RE ACTUALLY A PRICK

Without fail, this is a must. When you, a "city boy," move to a small town, people there will tend to regard you with a bit of trepidation. And it's *your* job to assuage all the fears they will inevitably have. Concerns that you're a fucking creep (which you are). Anxiety that you're trouble (which you also are). You need to immediately put them at ease by doing something amazing or engaging or so benevolent, that they can never again question your motives or actions. Such as . . .

THE FLORENCE NIGHTINGALE

Everyone has heard of the **Florence Nightingale effect**, named after that nutty nurse who picked up a lot of overtime shifts during wartime. Basically, it's when a caregiver has romantic feelings for a patient. The same can be applied to, say, a mysterious stranger. When you first arrive in town, find a way to hurt yourself, as in getting hit by a car or falling off a bridge. Whatever it is, just make sure it happens in public. Ideally with plenty of witnesses. Preferably choose something that won't accidentally kill you in the process. Then, what customarily happens in these small towns is that somebody will take you in and care for you. Help you recover. And that's when you've got 'em good.

A friendly stranger enters town.

This friendly stranger purposely gets
injured on Main Street.

The guilty driver takes in the friendly stranger
knowing nothing of his spending felonies.

The friendly stranger then gets extra
friendly with said vulnerable hausfrau.

THE ANONYMOUS HERO

The next confidence trick is very similar to the "beat up the bully" scam previously discussed. Much like how Shakespeare once said there were only seven types of stories, Pops always said there are only seven types of cons . . . just with multiple variations. This particular variation isn't going to make you a high-school hero. It will help you manipulate a town of twenty-five thousand or so people into taking you under their collective wing. And much like the bully gag, you'll need a **roper** for this one, too. The bit goes something like this: the roper picks a **shill** (remember—old lady, puppy, young kid) and does something terrible to the innocent victim (stealing a purse, kicking the dog, abducting the child—hey, get creative!). That's where you come in. The **courageous stranger** risking life and limb in defense of

Grandma, Lassie, or some pain-in-the-ass baby. And boom! You're *in* like Flintstone. And the more you resist the gratitude and reciprocation, the more it will come your way.

Scummy mugger attacks
a very frail old woman.

Courageous stranger comes out of
nowhere to fight off said crackhead.

Elderly victim thanks courageous
stranger, not knowing he actually paid to
have her beaten up.

Local paper lauds unknown hero because
local papers have never heard the phrase
"vetting your sources."

THE PHILANTHROPIST RECLUSE

And finally, the most difficult but most effectual variation is certainly the **philanthropist recluse**. Now, this one takes some doing, and it's not as easy as the aforementioned, but the chance of this one *sticking* in the long run is well worth the very detailed and seemingly extraneous setup. Trust me. There is a basic rule of the world that makes absolutely no sense: Rich people are given free shit while poor people starve. Why do you think famous athletes eat for free and Hollywood stars are constantly being given clothing and jewelry? Because they need it? Hell no, it's because they *don't*. If people don't think you want anything from them, *that's* the perfect front for robbing them blind. And this is the angle I chose for my visit to Honest, Indiana.

Same lazy local newspaper reporter is tipped off to rich stranger moving to town.

Rich stranger looks for a home to rent, wearing a Rolex and all the while spouting that annoying "giving back" bullshit.

Rich stranger makes a large donation to the local Kiwanis Club for god knows whatever the hell the Kiwanis Club does.

Town fetes rich stranger because the lives of these people are boring and empty and sad.

And that's literally what happened. The yokels of this town immediately made me an honorary Kiwanis member. Let me into their inner sanctum of tripe. And they didn't even fucking know me. Can you believe that? Yeah, me either. But you've gotta understand that in these little indistinguishable, flyover towns, being accepted quickly into an organization of that relative magnitude is equivalent to joining the fucking Illuminati. It doesn't get any bigger or more connected.

And in a place like Honest, Indiana, it was on par with getting the key to the goddamned city. Those rubes were already fucking cooked, and they didn't even know the oven was on.

There are a few other things necessary to get in good with the local townspeople. One of the most often forgotten, yet utterly important, is making the "town treasure" fall in love with you. Yes, I know it sounds clichéd and a bit absurd. And I know you've seen it in a million terrible movies. But the reason it's so familiar is because it's true. It's almost *essential* to success, or, at least, the impression of it. If the community darling fancies you, you are immunized against the rest of the residents who would normally like you less. It's almost like she's vetting *you* for *them*.

And, in my case, she would end up surprising *me* more than I ever thought possible.

HOW TO GET A "10" WHEN YOU'RE BARELY A "2 1/2"

This is one of the all-time-great questions asked by every man since they discovered fire and realized they had dicks. Novels, plays, movies—all have been dedicated to this one very specific topic. But what *I'm* going to do is pare it down to one small chapter of a picture book. I think that's the point, and it's part of why I'm writing this thing in the first place. Nothing, and I repeat, *nothing* in life is worth more than these few pages of your time. Teachers, priests, bosses—they'll try to intimidate you, try to convince you that all the things you want in life are difficult to attain and therefore demand all your time and effort. Again, this is just so you don't start a populist revolution and topple the powers that be or, at the very least, quit consistently stopping at red lights. Most importantly, teachers, priests, and bosses are perpetually full of shit—and ultimately the biggest con artists of them all. So please, if you do nothing else, always keep that in mind.

There are a few time-tested ways to con a woman into liking you. And don't kid yourself: whether you're nine or ninety, if you have a woman by your side, a con of some sort has certainly occurred. On your first date, when you didn't tell her about your sporadic bouts with E.D., con occurred. On your second date, when she didn't tell you she had four children from three different fathers, con occurred. On you. By you. Probably both. It happens. Now, I'm not going to write about the kinds of ways to get a girl interested in you that you might read in an online self-improvement blog. Ridiculous ones like "be confident" and "act bold/be bold"—or my personal favorite, "just ignore her." I don't know about you, but every time I've tried to ignore a woman in order to get her to like me, she just ignored me right back. No, the following are tangible, real-world ways to . . . Get. The. Girl. All for the means of working a longer con, of course (or in my case, something more).

DONATE TIME TO A CHARITY

Once you've settled into your new surroundings, you'll want to figure out what sort of charities the local "intelligentsia" support. Maybe it's farmers in need, if you're somewhere in Nebraska, or maybe it's an indigenous animal sanctuary, if you happen to be near the Everglades. Whatever it may be, find it. Pretend to give two shits about said cause. And more likely than not, this is where you'll come face to face with the local beauty queen. Because in every single one of these tiny enclaves, there's a town sweetheart that's the apple of everyone's eye. And nine times out of ten, she's volunteering at a shelter, handing out sandwiches to gross bums.

BE A WIDOWER

I don't care if you've got money, or a great job, or a *girthy member*—nothing turns a girl on more than a dead wife. Being a widower tells a woman, "Hey, I was married once, and through no fault of my own, that marriage has been rendered null and void." For a girl

you've just met, you've already been vetted by another, formerly living, woman. Obviously you weren't afraid of commitment. And depending on the contrived illness you give your made-up dearly departed spouse, you have shown your loyalty without ever having to do a damn thing. Mazel!

SAVE HER LIFE

This one is a derivative of some of the scams discussed earlier, but beneficial nonetheless. Again, you'll need a **roper** to play the attacker. Other than that, it's pretty simple. Now that you've established who the neighborhood sweetheart is (and again, I promise you, there's always a neighborhood sweetheart!), you wait for her to walk home from her job at the Ol' Steel Mill (or whatever terrible employment she's feigning contentment with), and just as the "assailant" jumps her, you pop out of nowhere, and with the karate you don't actually know, you beat the hell out of this hooligan and save her life. By the middle of the week, you'll be in her heart. By the middle of the month, you'll be in her pants.

PRETEND YOU'RE DYING

Chicks love this one, too. I call this the *Fault in Our Stars* syndrome. Women want the fairy tale, and more specifically the fairy tale where the guy dies at the end. Here's another secret nobody tells you: *love* is a scam, too. A *big* one. You see, people don't care about you when you're alive, but they'll cry their goddamned eyes out and put flowers on your grave when you're gone. Do you know why? Because we are born to be annoyed by each other. Because it's easier to like the revised memory of a wife or husband rather than the actual person that lived on Earth with you. The one who nagged you to be more romantic like the handsome guy from the movie, or the one who wished you made more money for the family like her ex on Facebook does. It's the same reason women marry men doing thirty to life behind bars. It's the perfect relationship for them, marrying the fantasy and not the felon. You don't believe me? Google these four words . . .

"Charles. Manson's. Hot. Girlfriend."

GET SOMEBODY TO VOUCH FOR YOU

Another instance where you will need a **roper**, but the most efficacious of the bunch, in my opinion. Choose somebody unassuming and trustworthy (cop, clergy, EMT) and get them to talk you up. Because when *you* do it, it's bragging, but when an elderly nun does it, it's charming. Get them to tell this girl how you saved a bunch of Russian orphans from an electrical fire in the flophouse they lived at. Or how you once raised $30K for a prosthetic limb so some one-legged kid in Botswana could finally play soccer with his thirty-five cousins. Next thing you know, *she'll* be approaching *you*.

And that's exactly what happened between me and Grace (not her name). She was actually the one who sought *me* out, believe it or not. I guess I had done so well exuding such great character in the town that she got fished up into my net of bullshit, too. And from the jump, I just knew that there was something special about this particular girl. She was smart, and funny, and had a sort of sneakiness of her own. The way she would get out of parking tickets with a coy smile. Or not pay for a refill at the movies by pretending she was deaf. All things she probably thought I didn't notice, but I did. And for a *mark*, I instantly had a connection with her. Not one that would get in the way of the con, mind you, but a connection nonetheless. Now, if I was a normal person with a heart and soul or any type of morals, I might even have considered dating her in the real world. Trust me, sometimes you can get stuck befriending some real unlikable assholes for the benefit of the con. But not with Samantha (not her name). She was beautiful. And funny. And smart. No, this was gonna be fun.

(Note: While this book might admittedly read a bit "straight man–centric," I want you all to know that women, gays, and even hermaphrodites can pull off these **rips**, too. Unlike most professions in our purported "country of meritocracy," **conning** is always an equal-opportunity employer.)

USING PEOPLE FROM YOUR PAST IN SHAMEFUL WAYS

You remember my dumb dad, right? The guy from the earlier chapters who used me in all of his flimflams and gave me exactly zero hugs total in my life? The one I keep talking about, even though I don't mean to? The one person with whom I ever had a "real" relationship in my life? Well, Pops finally got out of prison, and guess what? The ol' bastard decided to look me up. How he found me, I'll never know. But he did. And as it turned out, he hadn't changed a bit. He was his normal degenerate self. "Hey, sorry I missed your high-school graduation, dipshit. You know, the one that occurred over twenty years ago. That was my bad, bro." And he just happened to pop back into my life, NOT WHEN I NEEDED HIM, but rather right when I was about to pull off the *rook* of a lifetime. The one I'd been unwittingly planning from the minute he left me and told me he'd be back in a week or so.

You remember what I told you about *synchronicity*? Well, being the person that he was (a deep-down, straight-to-his-marrow creeper), the old prickstain wanted *in*. So I decided to use this new burden to my benefit. Suddenly, I became the "recluse philanthropist taking care of his aged father." (A disabled Grenada veteran. I know, so ridiculous. His idea.)

Now, at the time, I told myself I would allow him to stick around because I could take advantage of his advancing years. I could finally use him like he had used me as a child so many times before. But if I'm being really honest (which I almost never am), maybe . . . just maybe, I was happy to have the old fart around.

Anyway, as big of a pain in the ass as the old man could be, he actually proved to be quite helpful in *setting the table* to take this town for a ride. After all those years of being in the slammer, the old man wasn't rusty or tired or off his game even one bit. In fact, he was ready and raring to go. So the team was back together again. Me and Pops. And we'd attack this fleecing as a sort-of dynamic duo. Just like the old days. Hell, it's the least the jerk could do for me, right? After painting my childhood memories, not with *playful* times, but with *prison* time And even with all the anger and resentment I'd managed to collect since the last time we'd seen each other, I couldn't help but enjoy, just a little, the thought of us working together again. Like when the Eagles reunited for one more tour. Or when Hitler reunited with Mussolini in Vienna.

You know, come to think of it, maybe those childhood memories I had with my father weren't *all* bad ones.

You know, just most of them.

Pops made me wear those fucking bandages for a month.

PRETENDING TO LOVE YOUR FAMILY WHEN YOU REALLY DON'T

I know what you're thinking: "Jesus, how long is this long con gonna go on for?" The answer is, it goes on as long as it needs to go on. And starting a family is the next step in the plan. There are *tons* of ways to do this that don't include raising an *actual* family. Remember, when this is over, you'll be on the road, spinning hot dust on any and all people that were in your life just a few hours before, including your own children. And, much like getting the girl, having a family insulates you from the ever-peering gaze of collective distrust. People with families don't rob banks. A person with a wife and kids would never steal from the United Way's gimp fund. And most importantly, a man with a home full of loved ones would never even consider hoodwinking his entire community.

So, to start your instant family, pick one of the following . . .

MEET A WOMAN WHO ALREADY HAS CHILDREN

There is no creature more vulnerable on this earth than the single mother. And only a total fucking cad would take advantage of such a person in such a situation. That's how you know it's a quality hustle: only a disgusting, completely despicable person would actually lack the empathy to pull it off. And don't forget, you're not trying to be their new dad. Some of these little turds can be pretty resentful at first. *Your* move is to be the cool parent, and since you couldn't give two shits about their well-being or their prospective futures or any of that nonsense, this part should be easy. For example, you will let her little boy watch hardcore porno on your iPad. You will let her preteen girl dress like a Craigslist prostitute when she goes out at night to the mall. Shit, you'll even let them both burn doobies in the house (just as long as they share said doobies with you, of course).

For any shrewd con artist, this is child's play (literally). All in, it should only take you about a month or so to get these rug rats on your side. By letting them do whatever they want, you will get what *you* want: to have the kids on your team and to be known in the community as that wonderful fella who married Jane Smith and is acting like a father to her two bastard children. Taking these young tykes under your wing as if they were your own is the quintessential cover.

FOSTER A CHILD

Notice I didn't say *adopt*. When you try to adopt a kid under pretense (and believe me, I've tried), they make you fill out a bunch of useless paperwork and then do a ton of tedious interviews about why you have a burning desire to raise somebody else's mistake. But conversely, when you want to take in a *foster*, they check you for a pulse, make sure you're not a registered member of NAMBLA (The North American Man/Boy Love

Association—yes, it really exists), and then they deliver the little inbreed right to your door. Like you had just ordered an extra-large pizza with all the toppings. And if there is one thing that endears you to a community more than becoming a stepdad, it's becoming a foster dad. Most people don't want their own kids, let alone a stranger's. So kudos to you, friend!

Once the foster kid has arrived, you immediately need to parade him around town like he was a three-legged dog on fire. Oh, and make sure to get a kid with some color to him. White kids will always get you less sympathy, unless it's a white kid with a disability. Those are guaranteed money in the bank, too. The point being: the less socially desirable the child, the more advantageous it is as a cover. Again, be creative here!

HAVE AN ACTUAL BABY

Don't do this one. My own father disappeared on me constantly (as I've already stated numerous times). But as hard as he tried to unload me, he always ended up coming back. I mean, look where he ended up in this story so far. Back with me! I guess it's biological or something. Also, having your own kid just takes too long. Like nine months, from what I understand. So instead, you can just do what I did in Honest, Indiana . . .

PAY A JUVENILE DELINQUENT TO BE YOUR SON

The sidewalks are littered with people's forgotten dreams. They're also littered with homeless teens who'll do just about anything you could imagine for five hundred bucks. When you first pitch him (the street kid, I mean) that all he needs to do is move to some picturesque town, where he'll sleep in a warm bed, eat three square meals, and *not* get molested every night, he will be inherently skeptical. But after some convincing, and half the cash upfront, he'll be more than psyched.

Looking back on things, Tommy (not his real name) and I bonded almost immediately. He was a lot like me, when I thought about it. He had an "uncommon" upbringing. He faked his way through school. His dad was never around, and when he was, he was fucking horrible to him. Oh, and he had my eyes. Note: When you can choose between casting somebody as a **rube** or a **roper** (that means making somebody a teammate rather than an opponent), always go with the roper. Instead of trying to trick the kid, I got him on my side. Which, as it turns out, is way easier to do with somebody as street smart as a child hobo. Look, it's just human nature. If somebody has a monetary stake in a scam, then they're going to go above and beyond to make sure it goes off without a hitch. And that's exactly what little Gabe Jr. did (not his name).

Now, with my proverbial guns loaded, I was on my way. I had built a reputation as a sensational guy and a respectable family man. I hit all the boxes that are important to most of these simpleton types. I embodied all the nonsense that people believe *actually* matters in this world, like "character" and "loyalty" and "trust." Snooooooze. You see, to any accomplished con man, these aren't qualities. They are weaknesses. Vulnerabilities that need to be exploited, not celebrated. It's the American Way. If you recall, the Indians were an honorable and virtuous people, too. And look what good it did them.

That's why you want to be the Pilgrim in this life, and not the Indian. Everybody knows those gangster-ass Pilgrims were the *real* savages.

And if you really want to hold some sway over vast swaths of people, there's something else you need to do . . .

GET ELECTED TO SOMETHING AND ABUSE YOUR POWER

I n every facet of civilization, if you *make* the rules, then you're in the best position to *break* the rules. They say the most effective thieves in the world are the ones donning suits, not masks. This is also true for military uniforms, judges' robes, reverends' collars, and—don't delude yourself—the craven charlatans we elect every other November. You know, the ones who are supposed to protect us from all the supposed *bad* in society? My question is this: who the hell can we vote for to protect *us* from *them? No. Body.* I tell you this because if you ever start to feel guilty about following the guidance of this book, don't. Because for every scheme and deceit you've got running out in the world, the powers that be have got some ten thousand or more running back on you. *Karma, my nuts.*

Below I've listed a few ways to help get you into a power position in Small Town, USA. (Remember, the town can work as a placeholder for anything. You can swap it with a company, charity, social group, etc.)

GET ELECTED TO SOMETHING

Sorry to repeat myself, but among the least trustworthy people on earth, *politician* places at number two, right in front of *professional con man* and right behind *religious leader.* And in an arena this size, while the prestige may seem less, the access to the town's assets are greater (and dare I say more important). You see, being named constable, superintendent, or councilman is a big deal in one of these shit-kicker whistle stops. And that's because most dimwits want to be told what to do and how to live. Shit, we claim to be the "land of the free," but really we're the home of the "tell us what to think." From jewelry commercials to appointed officials. From unsubstantiated retweets to your racist uncle's email forwards. We

Americans love to be instructed as to what their opinions *should* be. So if you can achieve a level of power where you can use these inherent public weaknesses to your advantage, then you can steal everything from their Apple stocks to their knee socks.

START A NONPROFIT

Another thing people like, aside from being told what to do, is being told that *what* they do is good. Like my dad always said, "Playing into a person's pathetic self-worth is a great way to gain the upper hand with them, dipshit." And humans tend to believe that anyone who feeds the hungry or accompanies some inner-city throwaways to some shitty baseball game is *invariably* ethical, moral, and noble. And when you donate your hard-earned money to them or entrust your children with them, you assume they will do right by you. So in turn, you get to feel altruistic in absentia.

But truth be told, there are no Good Samaritans in today's world. And that's because there never really were any to begin with. People always look to get something for themselves out of the deal. Famous organizations that broadcast telethons or local nonprofits that ring their bells outside your supermarket—they all spend less than a quarter of your well-intentioned donations on the actual causes they're promoting. (And those are the good ones!) The rest of that money goes to "administrative costs," also known as: vacation homes, luxury sports cars, and droves of Honduran nannies.

So really, a "fake charity" is an oxymoron because, to one degree or another, they're all fake.

UNCOVER A MADE-UP CRISIS

One of my personal favorites. Outsider arrives in town to investigate a conspiracy and ends up miraculously saving the town, à la Erin Brockovich. This time you *will* need to say you're working for either the *New York Times* or the *Washington Post*, and

then chat up a few yokels. Inform them that you're there to do some secret under-cover research about fracking or carbon pollution or whatever currently en vogue environmental issue everyone's feigning concern over. And before long, you'll be speaking in front of their very own city council like it's the second-to-last scene in *Footloose*.

Or you could do what I did when I weaseled my way into the hearty embrace of the town that I was about to screw over. In Honest, Indiana, I chose to . . .

BECOME THE TOWN SAVIOR

What does that mean exactly, *town savior?* Well, in these economically uncertain times, it means *everything*. If you do a little research on the Internet, you will quickly find that most small towns are financially insolvent, primarily because of two things: (1) There is no middle class in America anymore, and (2) these towns are generally run by a group of idiots. The intelligent few that were unlucky enough to be born there either moved to a city of some distinction, or they shot themselves in the face with a pistol. And because of such events, these places are often left utterly vulnerable.

Which is how I was able to become a town savior in Honest. I established a non-profit that purportedly raised a ton of money to help local farmers in similar small towns (it did not). I exposed a major discrepancy in the local government's financial recordkeeping in respect to their farm subsidies (there was none). I formulated a plan to "resolve" the problem I had fucking made up in the first place! Then, I *officially* became the town savior when the mayor appointed me town comptroller. Because of my perceived business acumen and overtly honorable nature, Mayor Hamilton (not his name) decided to make me a person of authority in his precious little fiefdom. And voilà! I was in.

What is a comptroller, you ask? Well, while it sounds like the official title of your company's nerdy IT guy, it's a more powerful position than most people think. And those are *precisely* the gigs you want to be given. Low profile, high results. I want you to commit that last phrase to memory. **LOW PROFILE, HIGH RESULTS**. That one's a biggie.

Another important lesson to recognize is that the most important man in the world is *not* the president. No. It's the person who controls the president's staff. While the commander in chief is out shaking hands with the prime minister of

Canada and making speeches about the endlessly rising oceans and CO2 levels (neither of which he or she's ever *really* going to address), the gentleman or lady *behind* the president is the one actually running the country. The same is true of any small town. Everybody may want to be the mayor, but usually that asshole's biggest responsibility is cutting the ribbon at a new Target. Or judging the home-made marmalade contest at the county fair. Meanwhile, the seemingly less enviable position of town comptroller usually includes doing all of the bookkeeping. And by *bookkeeping*, I mean *laundering*. And by *laundering*, I don't mean your fucking dress shirts.

HOW TO EMBEZZLE MONEY AS A TOWN COMPTROLLER

Start a city bank account for something vaguely innocuous called a "renewal project."

Create a phony draft from the state paying for the project that you just made up.

Write a check out of that bank account to yourself, immediately "renewing" your lifestyle.

Disappear like a fart in the breeze before the inevitable citywide audit arrives.

If this all sounds simple, it's because, well . . . it is. Municipalities just don't have enough resources to support an effective checks-and-balances system. Which allows a person like me to write checks to himself and balance the difference on the ass of John Q. Taxpayer. Easy breezy. See, back when that mayor appointed me comptroller, (after the last one resigned in disgrace), he had no idea that he had just given me the combination to his safe. The key to his hope chest. The code to his little town's fucking ATM. It had all worked so perfectly, it stunned even *me*. And after I gained access, the cash was just sitting there, waiting to be taken. And I was the perfect one to do it. So I quickly created a fake "Community Parks Fund." The city council approved it without so much as taking a vote. And soon I was siphoning cash into the account, laundering it with no credible oversight, and filling my own personal till to my heart's content. Like I said, this shit was just too easy! My plan was working to perfection. My dad was back in my life. I had a hot girl by my side, who I actually liked! And for the first time in a long time, I felt like I belonged. And as cynical as I am, it felt pretty damn good, I must admit.

But as Pops always used to tell me, "Stealing the money ain't the hard part, dipshit. Hiding it—that's the real pickle."

REMEMBER NOT TO BE WHITE-TRASH RICH

A very quick way to get others to dislike you is to flaunt your wealth in their faces (see any show on the Bravo network). If you're swiping money from your boss, drive a beater to work. If you've squirreled away money from your ex-wife, certainly don't wear your new gold Submariner to the arbitration hearing. And if you're robbing every nickel from a place that's already deep in the hole, be sure to play more downtrodden than the lowly townspeople you supposedly represent.

I'm sure you're thinking, "A whole chapter on acting poor? 99 percent of the world acts poor every day—how hard can it be?"

Well, contrary to popular belief, it can be quite hard. These hustles can take a great deal of man-hours to fully perpetrate. During which time, after some of the green starts flowing in, you'll inevitably find yourself going crazy hankering to spend your winnings but knowing you'll get pinched if you do. (And you will *eventually* get pinched. Trust me on that one.) So here's a list of critical *dos* and *don'ts* to help you touch the money you've pilfered from others and still remain in their good graces. Again, I would argue that spending the money wisely is as, or more, difficult than looting it is. So . . .

Don't . . .

BUY A GIANT HOUSE

This is a total dickhead move that seems obvious to anybody with half a brain, but you'd be surprised how many idiots squander their first big score on an enormous abode they couldn't normally afford. It's this type of neophyte action that will get you busted a hundred out of a hundred times. We get it. You've lived in a dilapidated trailer your whole life and now you want to live it up. Well, you'll be living it up in a five-by-nine cell if you buy the *phatest crib* on the block, P. Diddy.

Do . . .

PIMP OUT A DUMP

Remember when you were young and grownups would say, "It's what's on the inside that counts?" While this was usually said to appease the ugly kids, it's especially true when it comes to enjoying a hustle. Find a sufficient place to squat. Then rent a U-Haul. Drive to a distant Costco. Fill the truck with the necessary amenities and accouterments that will make your stay in this toilet bowl of a town as comfortable as possible. Finally, pull into your new place of residence (or trailer park equivalent) and unload all of your goodies in the middle of the night.

Next, hire a couple of illegal aliens at a nearby Home Depot to wire, carry, or hang whatever you need wired, carried, or hung. (I specify "illegal aliens" here only because it's best to employ people who don't speak English in these types of situations; this allows you to hold *la migra* over their heads.)

Don't . . .

BUY A JERKOFF CAR

What's a jerkoff car? Simply put, anything with two seats, a price tag over $100,000, and/or ever owned by Jay Leno. The "Hey, look at me! I'm a total needle-dick!" rides. You know exactly what type of automobiles I'm talking about, so don't make me explain it. People only buy these cars because (1) they want their neighbors to feel worse about themselves than they already do, or (2) they have what medical doctors call "microphalluses." I've never really been a fan of the jerkoff car, per se. It's impractical. No room for groceries. And who cares if your whip can do 220 mph? You live in America, genius. Seventy-five is as much as we do here. There's no Autobahn to "open it up" on in Shithole, Missouri. But if you must have one of these ridiculous toys . . .

Do . . .

BUY A BEATER FOR THE WEEKDAYS

DRIVE A BENZ ON THE WEEKENDS

Being a total fraud in life takes supreme discipline. Most people aren't aware of that fact. They get in **The Game** thinking it's all VIP tables and bottles of Cristal. But you have to forever be thinking. Forever be *on*. Forever be on the lookout for something that might trip you up. And the one thing that will *inevitably* cause a misstep in your con man career (or as your average Regular Joe Fucktard on the street just trying to get by) is being yourself. Forget what your high school guidance counselor told you repeatedly during your senior year. Never, *ever* be yourself. It's the absolute worst thing you could do. Remember: *Honesty is NEVER the best policy*. So . . .

Don't . . .

UPGRADE YOUR LADY

This is a classic rookie move when a man ups his means (also the case when a woman tries to upgrade her fella, albeit less common because men are notoriously worse in this department). As much as you might want to jettison the average-looking wife or 5½ girlfriend who doesn't fit your current lifestyle, you must *not* do this. It's a giant red flag to those around you. People see a gross dude walking around with a supermodel, they draw one of two conclusions: (1) They're witnessing some sort of sanctioned kidnapping, or (2) the repugnant dude is stupid rich. So whatever you do, don't be the wealthy, ugly guy.

Do . . .

UPGRADE YOUR VACATIONS

I'm sure you've heard ad nauseam the phrase *What happens in Vegas stays in Vegaszzzzzz.* Excluding STDs and Drunk and Disorderlies, this corny saying happens to be completely true. It also holds true for most far-off destinations. I always go by the following steadfast rule: if you are going to cheat on your wife or spend money that you've "borrowed" from others, *without fail* do it at least three thousand miles away from your current home. Could be Hawaii. Could be Europe. Doesn't matter really. As long as you're doing it outside the continental US.

And finally, and most importantly in the dos and don'ts section . . .

Don't . . .

COUNT YOUR WINNINGS BEFORE THE HAND IS OVER

This one in particular strikes a very personal chord for reasons you will soon come to understand. If you start blowing your Super Bowl winnings during the shitty halftime show, don't be surprised when the other team comes out in the second half, an entirely new squad, and annihilates your ass by 13½. You see, this game is *continuously evolving*, and there will invariably be a *new* lesson to learn. And underestimating your mark is a lesson that could cost you. Bigtime.

Do . . .

ALWAYS ASSUME THE SUCKER IS ACTUALLY THE SNAKE

This is the *most important* rule of most important rules. And that's because it's the one that trumps all the others (kinda like how *thou shalt not kill* beats the adultery one). You must *constantly* assume that there are *other players in The Game*. No matter how ignorant the guy looks, no matter how friendly the woman acts, no matter how inviting the community appears to be, *always* expect the unexpected.

Note: More specifically, when you are picking a place to swindle, make sure they aren't setting you up to take the fall for a corrupt scam of their own.

SOMETIMES YOUR CON CAN BURN YOU BACK. LIKE HERPES.

Well, it seems there *was* a damn good reason why it all seemed way too easy. From getting the people to trust me. To getting the town sweetheart to fall in love with me. To being elected to higher office without ever having to engage in an actual election. And the reason it was so easy . . . was because it was intended to be. God, even writing about it now, I'm stunned at how dumb I was. ME! The best of the best . . .

. . . got burned by his own fire.

You see, as it turned out, most everybody in Honest, Indiana, wasn't so goddamned *honest* after all. From the mayor to the Kiwanis Club president to the local beauty queen—it seems they were *all* performing a con back on me. And in hindsight, all the telltale signs were there. I just failed to see them. Or, if I'm being totally honest with myself, perhaps I just didn't want to.

I should have noticed that kid mayor lived in a house way above his means.

Or that the president of the Kiwanis Club was clearly driving a jerkoff car.

And probably most embarrassingly, my main girl, the one I had fallen for so hard, that young and innocent soul I lovingly referred to as the "town treasure," the one I was *almost* willing to break character for . . .

. . . turns out she was secretly upgrading her guy, too.

As I came to find out (way too late, I might add), *they* were the ones who put that pop-up on the Internet, touting themselves as the "Most Honest Town in America." Not because they hoped it would attract more good people to their little town, but rather exactly *one* bad one. That ad was bait. For some creep from the big city. Some guy who thought he was way more clever than he actually was. A plan for that dickhead to come to town and *think* he could take these eighteen-thousand-plus people for a ride. But as fate would have it, the ride took me.

And that brings us back to the most peculiar pawn *in The Game*. Dear old Dad. Pops's fortuitous arrival came at a very suspect time, looking back. And though he denied it at first, I had the sneaking suspicion that he just *may* have had something to do with all of this. Shit, who am I kidding? I would have bet my life on it. All that "I'm proud of you" garbage. The stuff I so wanted to hear. The accolades that sounded so foreign coming out of his mouth. I should have known I was being played! And from the moment they took me away in those cuffs, I felt this awful gnawing in the base of my gut that said this "father" of mine acted as a *roper* to distract his only son . . . while an entire town pulled the scam of all scams . . . back on him.

Synchronicity, indeed.

Turns out the folks in Honest, Indiana, had been bleeding the place dry for a good decade or so. Everything I just showed you how to do—they had been doing for a long time before I ever got there. And right around the time I confidently sauntered across those city limits, they were just about to get a federal inquiry into why they had been in the red for so many years. So all they needed was a patsy to take the hit for them. A fall guy. Somebody who would know how to steal, embezzle, and misappropriate without ever batting an eye. What they needed was some greedy con man to do exactly what he did best.

And that con man was me.

But you know what the really curious part was? And this is going to sound fucking insane, but . . . I wasn't that angry about it. Not at all, in fact. On the contrary, I was actually impressed. And I was somehow comforted that there were not only a *few* like-minded people out in this world, but a whole goddamned congregation of them. An entire city, in fact! After a full lifetime of feeling like an outcast, a ship with no port, this place, this town of liars and scammers and crooks . . . actually felt kinda like home to me. My only real regret was that I wished I could have been part of the con, too. Wished I could have assisted my peers instead of being their target. But as those pussy French say, *c'est la vie, motherfucker.*

So if you are unfortunate enough to end up being burned by your own sham, by an entire city of shysters, and quite possibly by your own father, there's another quick chapter of lessons you need to memorize, ASAP . . . .

HOW TO PROTECT YOURSELF FROM A PRISON SEXUAL ASSAULT

One thing is for sure. If you decide to get into this business, no matter how clever you are, no matter how airtight the scheme, eventually one way or another you will be caught. It's just another part of *The Game*. (Like getting injured in football. Or criminally indicted as a Caucasian police officer.) Therefore, knowing how to survive behind bars is pertinent to your survival in *The Game*. Because if you're killed by an Aryan gang for sitting at the wrong chow table, your con artist career is officially over, and then what good are you? So I figured I'd add this last chapter because one day, sooner or later, you will find yourself behind similar walls (especially if you follow the lessons in this book). And you will need to be at the top of your game because these places are like Con Man Universities. And you are either taking classes or getting schooled (and perhaps raped). So . . .

BE HUMBLE

Remember when your highschool wrestling coach told you that there was always somebody tougher and meaner out there than you? Yeah, well, they all inhabit this locked compound. And one of them will most likely be your cellie.

DON'T BE CURIOUS

As much as it may look like it, you're not starring in a United Colors of Benetton commercial. You're not here to get to know anyone. Keep your mouth shut and your head down, and try to be invisible.

DON'T BE GANDHI

A repeated theme when you're growing up is "don't judge a book by its cover." We're taught not to see color, but to instead judge a person by the content of their character. Well, inside these razor wire fences, judge them by their color, lest ye be judged (and again, most likely raped).

DON'T ASSUME THE BEST IN PEOPLE

If you bum a smoke from a dude and he says, "It's a twofer," it means you now owe him two cigarettes for that one. Prison systems have their own economy. Out in the real world, people exchange money for goods and services. In prison, currencies called "cigarettes" and "drugs" are exchanged for services like "legal advice" and "blowjobs." Assume the worst in people. Always assume the worst.

BECOME A JAILHOUSE
F. LEE BULLSHITTER

The minute you can, head straight to the prison library. Do not pass Go. Do not collect $200. Spend all of your free time reading up on legal matters, specifically those that pertain to getting someone the fuck out of prison. Even if you know nothing about the law, advertise that you do.

PRETEND TO BE CRAZY

For a long time now, feigning mental illness has always been a great way for us humans to get out of trouble. From Howard Hughes to Mark David Chapman—the shit works. So your best bet is to try to be admitted into the psych ward. You'll have a much easier time there. And by that I mean there will be four cement walls between immediate danger and your butthole.

DON'T BE A SNITCH

If you see anything illegal going on—such as too many people congregating on the handball court or an inmate getting murdered with a pillowcase full of batteries—just walk away. The moment you snitch is the moment you become public enemy number two (right after the pillowcase beating guy). While you may have earned brownie points with the warden, you'll pay for it in severe ass whoopings later.

BIDE YOUR TIME

Now, here comes the good part. Keep your chin up! This is only your first offense. You won't catch life for scamming a few people. So spend your time inside wisely. Plan for what you're going to do when you get out. Use all those free moments to set up your next *angle*. And who knows? You just might get lucky. Your time behind bars could end up being a lot shorter than you would have anticipated. You see, sometimes the people you've always counted on the *least* . . . end up being the ones who are there for you when you need them *most*. If you don't believe it, I have proof.

You see, it was Pops who got the town to hire a really smart city attorney. It was my dad who came up with the ingenious plan of getting me out of prison on a technicality. It was my FATHER, the one that had betrayed me, who got everybody in Honest, Indiana, to refuse to testify against me. And if you know anything about the law (and being a former fake lawyer, I knew this well), you know that when no one is willing to testify against you, it's kinda hard for the federal government to build a credible case.

So instead of seeing me locked away for good and letting me rot, my father talked the town into another option. And after some nudging by him, the people of Honest, Indiana, had a proposition for me. To join them. In the hopes of making their town a veritable SPIDER'S WEB OF CON. They saw how good I was at what I did. Saw my potential. Figured they could use me. And after the heat died down a little, and with the help of dear ol' Dad, they decided to recruit me to catch the next batch of swindlers, charlatans, and crooks. The next *marks* that would inevitably be coming to Honest, Indiana, ready and willing to take advantage of it. To roll it. To try to leave *their* mark, as I had done before them. And do you know what I did, without hesitation? I said yes. It seems after all that I had gone through, even going to prison, I couldn't deny that this town was where I belonged.

My dad did all that for me.

Do you remember early on when I told you this book was a sort of love story? About two people who, after all that difficult stuff went down between them, you could never imagine ending up together at the end . . . *actually* ending up together?

Nah, I wasn't talking about the local sweetheart. She still sucks.

I was actually talking about my dad.

As it turns out, he *was* proud of me. And in the end, that's all I ever really wanted. That's all any of us ever want; whether we deny it or not, it's just true. And it also turns out that this *really* is an apt title to my book. Because I did "*Win at Life.*" Just not the way I had expected to. And that's how it usually works, right?

If you're lucky, that is. Thanks, Pops.

My plan working to perfection.

ENOUGH WITH THE BOOK. GO SCAM SOMEONE.

Now you know the basics. The ups and downs. The ins and outs. The fundamentals of **The Game**. I hope this book was helpful to you in some way. Maybe it taught you to be more cynical and less of a target. Maybe it taught you how to *find* a target. Maybe you just occasionally flipped through it while *deucing*. I don't really give a hot damn which it was. Because in the end, all proceeds of this book will benefit the Foundation for Underprivileged Kids United. A nonprofit I'm proud to endorse here and now. You see, I had a revelation after I finished writing. *This* was going to be the *only* way I would be able to give back to the world after I had taken so much from it. And I know this is going to sound corny . . . but if I can help just one kid get off the streets . . . protect one child so he or she is not raised the same way I was . . . then all of this would have been worth it.

I'm lying. That acronym is FUK U. But if you've been paying *any* attention, then you already knew that, didn't you?

Besides, unless their last name is Rowling, nobody is making a profit writing some dumb book these days. No, I'm just hoping this turns into a TV show or movie or something. I'm not making squat any other way. So, what the hell are you waiting for, dipshit?

Steal the fucking book . . .

ABOUT

THE AUTHOR

As the inaugural member of The Walt Disney Studios Writers' Program, Mark Perez has been writing professionally for twenty years. In that time, he's sold over twenty-five screenplays to the likes of Universal, MGM, Warner Bros., New Line, and Columbia, among others. He's also written pilots for ABC, NBC, FOX, Comedy Central and more, and written projects for Adam Sandler, Steve Martin, Ben Stiller, and Diane Keaton, among others. His next movie, *Game Night*, starring Jason Bateman and Rachel McAdams, is being produced by Warner Bros. and New Line, and will be released Valentine's Day weekend in 2018.

THE CARTOONIST

For forty-five years, Scott Shaw! has written and drawn underground comix (*Fear and Laughter*), kids' comic books (*Captain Carrot And His Amazing Zoo Crew!*, *Sonic The Hedgehog*, *Simpsons Comics*), comic strips (*Woodsy Owl*), graphic novels (*Annoying Orange*), TV cartoons (*Jim Henson's Muppet Babies*, *Camp Candy*, *The Completely Mental Misadventures of Ed Grimley*), and advertising (Pebbles Cereal starring The Flintstones), and was one of the kids who started the San Diego Comic-Con—so he knows all about getting conned.

THE PHOTOGRAPHER

Annastasia Goldberg really should know better than to hang out with miscreants like the gentlemen listed above, but the book's editor made her an offer she couldn't refuse, and it led her down the dark path to perdition. A graduate from UCLA in Fine Arts, she has provided photography for *Variety* magazine and the *Los Angeles Times*, and currently focuses on artistic portraiture. She has never accepted any wooden nickels.

Little Lulu

CREATIVE GIANTS!

GET YOUR FIX OF DARK HORSE BOOKS FROM THESE INSPIRED CREATORS!

MESMO DELIVERY SECOND EDITION - Rafael Grampá

Eisner Award–winning artist Rafael Grampá (*5*, *Hellblazer*) makes his full-length comics debut with the critically acclaimed graphic novel *Mesmo Delivery*—a kinetic, bloody romp starring Rufo, an ex-boxer; Sangrecco, an Elvis impersonator; and a ragtag crew of overly confident drunks who pick the wrong delivery men to mess with.

ISBN 978-1-61655-457-6 | $14.99

SIN TITULO - Cameron Stewart

Following the death of his grandfather, Alex Mackay discovers a mysterious photograph in the old man's belongings that sets him on an adventure like no other—where dreams and reality merge, family secrets are laid bare, and lives are irrevocably altered.

ISBN 978-1-61655-248-0 | $19.99

DE:TALES - Fábio Moon and Gabriel Bá

Brazilian twins Fábio Moon and Gabriel Bá's (*Daytripper*, *Pixu*) most personal work to date. Brimming with all the details of human life, their charming tales move from the urban reality of their home in São Paulo to the magical realism of their Latin American background.

ISBN 978-1-59582-557-5 | $19.99

THE TRUE LIVES OF THE FABULOUS KILLJOYS - Gerard Way, Shaun Simon, and Becky Cloonan

Years ago, the Killjoys fought against the tyrannical megacorporation Better Living Industries. Today, the followers of the original Killjoys languish in the desert and the fight for freedom fades. It's left to the Girl to take down BLI!

ISBN 978-1-59582-462-2 | $19.99

DEMO - Brian Wood and Becky Cloonan

It's hard enough being a teenager. Now try being a teenager with *powers*. A chronicle of the lives of young people on separate journeys to self-discovery in a world—just like our own—where being different is feared.

ISBN 978-1-61655-682-2 | $24.99

SABERTOOTH SWORDSMAN - Damon Gentry and Aaron Conley

When his village is enslaved and his wife kidnapped by the malevolent Mastodon Mathematician, a simple farmer must find his inner warrior—the Sabertooth Swordsman!

ISBN 978-1-61655-176-6 | $17.99

JAYBIRD - Jaakko and Lauri Ahonen

Disney meets Kafka in this beautiful, intense, original tale! A very small, very scared little bird lives an isolated life in a great big house with his infirm mother. He's never been outside the house, and he never will if his mother has anything to say about it.

ISBN 978-1-61655-469-9 | $19.99

MONSTERS! & OTHER STORIES - Gustavo Duarte

Newcomer Gustavo Duarte spins wordless tales inspired by Godzilla, King Kong, and Pixar, brimming with humor, charm, and delightfully twisted horror!

ISBN 978-1-61655-309-8 | $12.99

SACRIFICE - Sam Humphries and Dalton Rose

What happens when a troubled youth is plucked from modern society and thrust though time and space into the heart of the Aztec civilization—one of the most bloodthirsty times in human history?

ISBN 978-1-59582-985-6 | $19.99

AVAILABLE AT YOUR LOCAL COMICS SHOP OR BOOKSTORE
To find a comics shop in your area, call 1-888-266-4226. For more information or to order direct: ON THE WEB: DarkHorse.com
E-MAIL: mailorder@darkhorse.com / PHONE: 1-800-862-0052 Mon.–Fri. 9 a.m. to 5 p.m. Pacific Time.

EMPOWERED

VOLUME 1
ISBN 978-1-59307-672-6 $17.99

VOLUME 2
ISBN 978-1-59307-816-4 $16.99

VOLUME 3
ISBN 978-1-59307-870-6 $16.99

VOLUME 4
ISBN 978-1-59307-994-9 $16.99

VOLUME 5
ISBN 978-1-59582-212-3 $16.99

VOLUME 6
ISBN 978-1-59582-391-5 $15.99

VOLUME 7
ISBN 978-1-59582-884-2 $16.99

VOLUME 8
ISBN 978-1-61655-204-6 $16.99

VOLUME 9
ISBN 978-1-61655-571-9 $17.99

VOLUME 10
ISBN 978-1-50670-414-2 $19.99

EMPOWERED
UNCHAINED VOLUME 1
ISBN 978-1-61655-580-1 $19.99

EMPOWERED
DELUXE EDITION
VOLUME 1 hardcover
ISBN 978-1-59582-864-4 $59.99

EMPOWERED
DELUXE EDITION
VOLUME II hardcover
ISBN 978-1-59582-865-1 $59.99

EMPOWERED
DELUXE EDITION
VOLUME III hardcover
ISBN 978-1-50670-452-4 $59.99

AVAILABLE AT YOUR LOCAL COMICS SHOP OR BOOKSTORE.
TO FIND A COMICS SHOP IN YOUR AREA, CALL 1-888-266-4226

EVAN DORKIN

EISNER AND HARVEY AWARD WINNER

OMNIBUS COLLECTIONS FROM DARK HORSE BOOKS